and the I.R.S.

A Comedy in Three Acts

by William Van Zandt
& Jane Milmore

A SAMUEL FRENCH ACTING EDITION

SAMUEL
FRENCH
FOUNDED 1830
New York Hollywood London Toronto
SAMUELFRENCH.COM

ISBN 978-0-573-61196-4   Printed in U.S.A.   #14123

IMPORTANT BILLING AND CREDIT REQUIREMENTS

LOVE, SEX AND THE I.R.S. was first performed June 1, 1979, at the Dam Site Dinner-Theatre, Tinton Falls, New Jersey, under the direction of William Van Zandt. It was produced by Denis Lynch and Kathy Reed. Set and lighting were by Russell Schiavone. Sound was by De John Judson. The cast, in order of appearance, was as follows:

KATE DENNIS . . . . *Jane Milmore*

LESLIE ARTHUR . . . . *Billy Van Zandt*

MR. JANSEN . . . . *Drew Hollywood*

JON TRACHTMAN . . . . *Tom Frascatore*

FLOYD SPINNER . . . . *Don Brennan*

VIVIAN TRACHTMAN . . . . *Emi Hemleb*

CONNIE . . . . *Pam D'Amato/Maureen Milmore*

ARNOLD GRUNION . . . . *Frank Wolverton*

Love, Sex, and the I.R.S.

ACT ONE
SCENE 1

AS CURTAIN RISES, we see a present-day bachelor apartment in Manhattan. Stage Right, we see an archway which leads to an off-stage kitchen. U.S.R. *is the front door. All along the back we see a skylight, complete with a view obstructed by clothes-lines. Stage Left has a landing which leads upstairs to the bedrooms. Center Stage is a comfortable-looking sofa. On it, we see* LESLIE ARTHUR, *a gawky young man in his early twenties. He is engaged in a passionate kiss with* KATE DENNIS, *a pretty little brunette.* LESLIE *tries to break the kiss and speak.* KATE *fights him.*

KATE. No, Leslie!

LESLIE. Why not?

KATE. The wedding's not for two weeks. What's the rush?

LESLIE. Oh, come on, Kate.

KATE. No. It can wait.

LESLIE. It cannot wait. Believe me, it cannot wait.

KATE. (*Kissing him all over.*) Is that all you can think about?

LESLIE. At the moment? Yes. (*Finally.*) When are you going to tell Jon that you can't marry him?

KATE. The wedding's not for two weeks! I'll fit it in there somewhere. (KATE *attempts another passionate kiss.* LESLIE *stops her.*)

LESLIE. Wait. Wait. Wait a minute. Time out. Kate,

5

don't you realize that in two weeks you will be married to Jon?

KATE. Of course I do. I'm engaged to him. (KATE *tries another kiss*. LESLIE *moves away from her*.)

LESLIE. Kate, would you stop? (LESLIE *begins pacing*.) I'm not sure if you noticed, but we've been sneaking around behind his back for almost a week now. I just had some proof of it on the couch a second ago.

KATE. I'm aware of what we do on the couch, Leslie. I just can't bring myself to tell him.

LESLIE. Well, you're going to have to tell him. Two weeks from now, when the three of us go on our honeymoon, it'll probably be too late.

KATE. Why haven't you told him? You're his best friend!

LESLIE. Look, I'm a nervous wreck whenever we're all together. I can't look Jon in the eye anymore. I even feel guilty when I lay on the couch.

KATE. Lie on the couch! All we've ever done together was lie on the couch!

LESLIE. I was planning on getting around to more. Look, I've tried to bring up the subject to Jon but I get scared.

KATE. Scared of what?

LESLIE. Well, back in college I tried to tell him that his girlfriend was fooling around with one of his professors. The same thing happened. I got scared. My mouth dried up and nothing came out. Jon never knew what the reason was. He just figured I had a sinus problem. It's a good thing I didn't tell him. The jerk that did was attacked. Jon went crazy in the guy's dorm and broke everything.

KATE. Like what?

LESLIE. His arm, his leg, a few ribs . . .

KATE. You're talking about Jon Trachtman?

LESLIE. Yes, I'm talking about Jon Trachtman. When he finished with the guy, they had to wheel him into surgery. On four separate tables. And you should have seen what he did to his guide dog!

KATE. That's terrible.

LESLIE. And mind you, this is just the guy that told him. The professor . . .

KATE. I'd rather not hear it. What happened to the girl?

LESLIE. I don't know. No one ever saw her on campus again. Rumor has it that she joined a convent.

KATE. I know how it is, Leslie. It's hard telling Jon I want to break up when he keeps calling me his "little Moonpie."

LESLIE. "His 'little Moonpie?' "

KATE. He likes Moonpies.

LESLIE. I think we have a problem, Kate.

KATE. It's not easy telling your fiance that your in love with his best friend, either.

LESLIE. Keep your voice down. The neighbors have very thin walls and very big mouths. I think it's better if he suspects nothing until we can break it to him gently.

KATE. If we wait any longer, he's going to walk in here, catch us together and we won't have to say anything.

LESLIE. (*Looking at watch.*) Omigod, what time is it? Get out of here, before he comes home. (LESLIE *begins shoving* KATE *towards the door.*)

KATE. You're not very adventurous. Getting caught together could be very romantic.

LESLIE. If you want adventure, go walk through the Bronx during a gang war. I'll call you later. (KATE *barely gets into her coat as* LESLIE *pushes her. Just as they reach the door, we hear the DOORBELL.*) Who can that be? Are you expecting anybody?

KATE. Leslie, I don't even live here!

LESLIE. Then who's out there?

KATE. I don't know!

LESLIE. You don't suppose Jon forgot his key or something?

KATE. You think it's him? I don't want him to see me here. What should I do?

LESLIE. Hide. Just hide. (*The DOORBELL rings again.*
LESLIE *and* KATE *are frantic.*)
KATE. Where?
LESLIE. The closet!
KATE. There is no closet.
LESLIE. What?
KATE. You don't have a closet!
LESLIE. You're kidding.
KATE. Leslie!
LESLIE. Oh. Then, I'll open the door with you cleverly
hidden behind it. And when he comes inside you can sneak
out.
KATE. All right.

(KATE *hides behind the door.* LESLIE *composes himself,
opens the door and there before us is not Jon at all, but*
MR. JANSEN, *a beer-bellied drunk of a landlord. He
holds a beer can in one hand and an opened telegram
in the other.* LESLIE *is glued to the doorknob as*
JANSEN *enters.* KATE *is hidden from view behind the
opened door, against the* U.C. *wall.*)

LESLIE. Oh! Mr. Jansen, what a relief!
JANSEN. What happened, the toilet back up again?
LESLIE. No. I'm just glad to see you.
JANSEN. You are? What's going on? Do you have drugs
in here?
LESLIE. Of course not.
JANSEN. You keeping a broad in here?
LESLIE. What makes you think that?
JANSEN. You're acting too nice. I don't like it when
people are nice to me. What are you hiding?
LESLIE. Nothing.
JANSEN. Let me just look around here. (*As* JANSEN
snoops around, LESLIE *slams the door against the wall to
keep* KATE *hidden from view.*) You got the place looking
pretty good.

LESLIE. Thanks. You should see it from the outside.

JANSEN. What happened to that big hole in the ceiling that used to be right up there?

LESLIE. Oh. It's still there. But the guy upstairs bought a rug.

JANSEN. Is that so? (KATE *tries to sneak out and* LESLIE *smashes her into the wall as* JANSEN *walks by.*) Yup, this place looks pret-ty good. Don't make it look too good, though, or I'll start raising your rent.

LESLIE. That's why I didn't want you to come in. The place looks so good, I was afraid you'd want to raise our rent.

JANSEN. It doesn't look that good. (*Again,* KATE *tries to escape and is slammed into the wall.*)

LESLIE. Well, so long Mr. Jansen. Thanks for barging in . . . dropping in.

JANSEN. (*Heads for the door.*) Yeah. What are you, practicing to be a door man or something? (*He laughs.* LESLIE *follows and laughs also.*)

LESLIE. Doorman . . . ha ha . . . that's very funny. "Practicing to be a doorman." Yessir, that's pretty funny.

JANSEN. It's not that funny. (JANSEN *exits.* LESLIE *shuts the door.* KATE *is plastered against the wall.*)

LESLIE. Oh, Kate, I'm sorry. Are you okay?

KATE. I don't think I can ever give birth. But aside from that, I'm fine.

LESLIE. Here, why don't you sit down for a minute.

KATE. Thank you.

LESLIE. But just a minute. You've got to get out of here. (KATE *is seated on the couch as* JANSEN *enters with a pass key.*)

JANSEN. Aha!

LESLIE. Mr. Jansen, while you're here, would you mind fixing the doorbell? I think it's broken.

JANSEN. What is this? What do I see? What am I seeing?

LESLIE. It's nothing. You're drinking too much again. It's a hallucination!

JANSEN. Nice try. But my hallucinations are blonde. Who's the broad, Leslie? Why were you hiding before? You living here now?

KATE. No sir, I'm not.

JANSEN. Then why were you hiding?

LESLIE. She was hiding because we thought it might be you at the door and we didn't want to give you the wrong impression. Sir.

JANSEN. Oh? Good. Married or another building. That's my motto.

LESLIE. Good motto. Mr. Jansen, I'd like you to meet Kate Dennis.

JANSEN. Pleased to meet you.

KATE. I think we've met before.

JANSEN. Yeah? Doesn't matter, cause I don't remember you. Who's girl are you? Jon's or Leslie's?

LESLIE. That's hard to say right now.

JANSEN. What?

KATE. What Leslie means to say is that I'm Jon's fiancee.

JANSEN. Oh, yeah, I got a telegram here for Jon. I almost forgot. You sure you're not living here now?

LESLIE. Mr. Jansen, you're free to search the apartment anytime you like.

JANSEN. Okay, I'll take you up on that sometime. You're a witness, Carol.

LESLIE. Fine. Now what about the telegram?

JANSEN. It's from Chicago. They delivered it before and nobody was home. So I took it for you.

LESLIE. What's it say?

JANSEN. It says that . . . how should I know. (JANSEN *hands over the telegram and exits, leaving the door open.*)

LESLIE. I wonder who this is from.

KATE. What gives your landlord a right to be so nosey?

LESLIE. We're two months behind in the rent. He can be as nosey as he wants.

KATE. Well, I'd better get out of here, while I have the chance.

LESLIE. Yeah. Get out of here.

(KATE *turns to leave and in through the open door, walks* JON: *good-looking, in his early twenties, very likeable. He carries some sheet music under his arm.*)

KATE. Jon!

LESLIE. Oh boy! (*The telegram flies out of his hand to somewhere behind the bar.*)

JON. Hi Katie. What's new?

KATE. Uh . . . tell him, Leslie. (LESLIE *makes dry-mouth noises.*)

JON. Leslie, what's the matter? God, I haven't heard those noises since college. (LESLIE *tries to speak again. All that escapes his lips is a low moan.*) Christ, Leslie. You sound like a drowning moose. Do you want some water?

LESLIE. Kate . . . grblagh . . . Kate came to see you.

JON. I know that. Now relax. Why don't you sit down.

LESLIE. No, I'm fah . . . I'm fah . . . I'm fah . . .

JON. Leslie used to have these sinus attacks in college. Remember Leslie?

LESLIE. Umm . . . hmm . . .

JON. They used to come at the strangest times. I'm sorry you're not feeling well, Leslie, I wanted to take you both out to celebrate.

KATE. Celebrate what?

JON. It's taken me three months, but I finally got our band a booking.

KATE. Oh. Oh, that's wonderful. Isn't that wonderful Leslie?

LESLIE. Wonderful.

JON. I thought you'd be more thrilled than that. Now, come on, you'll never guess where.

KATE. Max's Kansas City?

JON. Nope.

KATE. Uh . . . C.B.G.B.'s?

Jon. Nope.

Kate. We give up. Where?

Jon. Weehawkan. The Huderwitz Bar Mitzvah.

Leslie. You're right. We never would've guessed.

Jon. Look, it's money, Leslie.

Kate. Of course we'll celebrate the Huderwitz Bar Mitzvah.

Jon. Great. Where will it be? Nathan's or Blimpie's?

Kate. Blimpie's is fine with me.

Jon. You gonna come with us, Leslie? (Leslie *makes more noises.*) Leslie, are you going to come with us?

Leslie. No. No. I have a lot to do today.

Jon. Like what?

Leslie. Well, I was thinking of having my sinuses drained. And I have to practice for the bar mitzvah.

Jon. It's not until next October.

Leslie. But I haven't played in a couple weeks. I wouldn't want to let the Huderwitzes down.

Jon. Okay, Leslie. Well, Katie, I guess it's just you and me, right little Moon Pie?

Leslie. On second thought I think I'll come.

Jon. All right. Just let me change and we'll go. I spent the whole morning trying to teach little Georgie Leach to play a scale on the tuba. Another six months and he might get it. (Jon *loosens his tie and exits to the bedrooms.*)

Leslie. All right. Don't panic. He suspects nothing. Thank God he didn't go to the bar. I forgot to wipe your lipstick off the glasses. Now he'll never know.

Kate. What? That I drink? Take it easy.

Leslie. I can't go on like this. Can't we tell him? Please can't we tell him? Maybe if we all sit down and discuss this like rational human beings?

Kate. What about that guy in school you were just telling me about?

Leslie. Well, that probably occurred because the guy didn't know what he was in for. I know what we're in for.

As long as . . . (LESLIE *begins bouncing around the room like a lunatic boxer as he speaks and continues this throughout the following dialogue.*) I handle this rationally and intellectually like a level-headed rational intellectual . . .

KATE. What are you doing?

LESLIE. It's very hard to hit a moving target. We'll just say, "Jon, Kate and I have something to tell you, old buddy." I hope my Maypo stays down. We'll say, "Jon . . ." (JON *re-enters. He's changed into a pair of jeans and sport shirt.*)

KATE. Jon!

JON. What?

LESLIE. Oh boy . . . Okay, Jon . . . (*Noises.*)

JON. What are you doing, Leslie?

LESLIE. Okay, Jon, old buddy . . . (*Noises.*)

JON. Kate, what is he doing?

KATE. Tell him, Leslie.

LESLIE. (*Noises.*)

JON. What's wrong with you? Kate, what's wrong with him?

KATE. Uh . . . it's his sinuses, I guess.

LESLIE. Thanks a lot, Kate. (*Noises.*)

(*The TELEPHONE rings, as* JON *goes to answer it,* LESLIE *continues bouncing around.*)

JON. Leslie, jumping around like that isn't going to clear up your nose. Now, don't encourage him, Kate. (JON *answers the phone,* LESLIE *continues bouncing.*) Hello? . . . Yes, this is Jon Trachtman . . . who? . . . Leslie, do you mind? (LESLIE *winds down and stops.*) Thank you . . . (*Into phone.*) I'm sorry. What can I do for you, Mr. Spinner? . . . Yes, I'll be home all day tomorrow. . . . I'm afraid that I don't understand. . . . what? . . . oh, my wife? (LESLIE *and* KATE *exchange looks.*) . . . Yes, of course . . . One o'clock will be fine . . . Yes, see you then. (JON *hangs up, stunned. After a slight pause.*)

KATE. Your what?

LESLIE. I thought I heard you say something about a wife . . .

JON. I did.

KATE. You haven't got a wife. Have you?

JON. Let me put it this way. It would have made things easier.

LESLIE. You can say that again.

KATE. It would have made what easier?

JON. Kate, would you mind going home now?

KATE. Brother, you sure wear out your welcome quick around here.

LESLIE. What's going on?

KATE. Are you in some kind of trouble?

JON. I need time to think, please go home Katie.

KATE. I will not go home. I'm marrying you in two weeks, I think I have a right to know what's wrong.

LESLIE. Yes Jon, Moon Pie and I have a right to know what's wrong.

JON. All right. It has to do with my taxes.

LESLIE. What? Who was that on the phone?

JON. A man named Floyd Spinner. From the Internal Revenue Service.

LESLIE. Wait a second. You told the I.R.S. that you were married?

JON. No. I did not tell the I.R.S. that I was married.

LESLIE. Good.

JON. I told the I.R.S. that we were married.

LESLIE. You told the I.R.S. that we were married? We who? We-You and me—We?

JON. Yes, kind of . . .

LESLIE. Kind of? I'm a man. Did you tell them that you were married to a man?

KATE. I don't get it. How could they get the idea that you

two were married? Who's the idiot who does your tax returns every year?

JON. I do my own, thank you.

KATE. What about you, Leslie?

LESLIE. My accountant does mine.

KATE. Oh? Who's your accountant?

LESLIE. Jon.

KATE. How did they get the impression that you were married to Leslie?

JON. I told them.

KATE. You told them that you were married to a man?

JON. No, I did not tell them I was married to a man.

KATE. What did you tell them?

JON. I told them I was married to a woman.

KATE. You told them you were married to a woman?

JON. Yes. I changed his sex. They kind of think Leslie's a woman.

LESLIE. They kind of think I'm a what?

KATE. Woman.

LESLIE. I heard him. They kind of think I'm a what?

JON. Look, Leslie could very easily be a man's name or a woman's name. I saved us a lot of money this way. Remember what it was like four years ago? Kate, you don't know. It was embarrassing. Every two weeks Leslie would get his hair cut at the A & P. In the meat department. To this day, whenever I smell calves liver I comb my hair. And me, I walked around with contact paper on my shoes. Something had to be done. Do you know how humiliating it is to have to take in laundry? From other people's clothes-lines? We needed a way out. Then, I found out that simply by changing our status to married, we could keep a lot of what we'd normally pay in taxes. Even if we did pay it, the government would only waste it anyway. It was so easy. And after getting away with it the first year, I figured I could keep on doing it. Who would think they'd catch us?

LESLIE. I would. Right now. I think they caught us.

KATE. Now what are you going to do?

JON. I'm thinking. This could be very serious, you know. Four years. Four years, I've been cheating the government out of money they don't deserve in the first place. This country was founded as a revolt against high taxes and now here we are with the I.R.S. coming to investigate us.

LESLIE. Us? Again with the us? Isn't it obvious that I'm not a woman? It's going to be a very quick investigation, isn't it? Isn't it?

JON. Not necessarily . . .

KATE. What are you thinking?

JON. I'm not sure.

KATE. You don't think you can pull something like this off, do you?

JON. Yes, I do. They have no complaints with my book-keeping, just my claim of Leslie's sex. I'll simply doctor up all of Leslie's I.D. and get this Spinner guy so drunk he can't see straight.

KATE. But he's going to want to see your wife.

JON. Of course he's going to want to see my wife. That's where you come in.

KATE. Me?

LESLIE. Yeah.

JON. I'll need some of your clothes to drape around here.

LESLIE. Yeah.

JON. And I'll need a couple of girlie items to make the place look lived in by a woman.

LESLIE. Yeah.

JON. And I'll need something for Leslie to wear.

LESLIE. No. What do you mean for Leslie to wear? Why can't Kate be Leslie?

JON. No. She's the wrong size. She has different colored eyes. And we all know she can't keep a secret.

KATE. That's what you say.

JON. If anything goes wrong, it'll mean a large fine to pay. And we haven't got enough to pay the rent. Or else it means a prison sentence. No. The only way to pull this off is for you to be yourself, Leslie. Your female self.

LESLIE. No. I am not dressing up like any woman. Forget it, you can just go to jail, pal.

JON. Fine. But your name is on those forms too. If I go to jail, you go to jail with me. Pal.

LESLIE. (*After a pause.*) What time is he coming?

JON. Good boy, thank you Leslie. Now, let's go eat. After you ladies . . .

END ACT ONE—SCENE ONE

ACT ONE
SCENE 2

It is the next morning, around eleven o'clock. We find JON *at coffee table with wads of papers. Erasers and pens of assorted types are strewn over top of everything. The apartment has obviously been re-decorated by* KATE. *Brightly colored throw pillows, plants and flowers, lace tablecloths, scatter rugs have all been added. It looks clean.* JON *is dressed rather collegiately and cool as can be. He touches up some document and rises, crossing to the bedrooms. He calls off.*

JON. Leslie, are you sure this is all of your I.D.?

LESLIE. (*Enters from the bedrooms. He is getting nervous. As he speaks he applies make-up to cover his five o'clock shadow.*) Yes. Have you finished touching them up? It's almost eleven-thirty.

JON. All done. Now relax. Mr. Spinner won't be here until one.

LESLIE. (*Evens his "base" by applying the make-up to the rest of his face.*) What are you doing with my draft card?

JON. I'm burning it. There's no draft anymore. You don't need it.

LESLIE. They must have it on file somewhere.

JON. Relax. He's not going to ask to see my wife's draft card. He thinks you're a woman. Trust me.

LESLIE. That's what you said when you said "Let me do your taxes."

JON. Hey, let's not rub my nose in this.

LESLIE. That's easy for you to say. You're not powdering yours.

JON. What does that mean?

LESLIE. You don't even feel guilty, do you?

JON. No.

LESLIE. (*Applying the last of the make-up.*) Here I am. My life passing from one sex to the other, right before my eyes. And you don't even feel guilty.

JON. No. I don't. Did Kate bring the clothes over?

LESLIE. Yes. And I'm not wearing them.

JON. All right. I do feel guilty. Now, will you wear them?

LESLIE. No.

JON. Leslie, you have to wear them. We can't ask Mr. Spinner to pretend, can we?

LESLIE. I just don't think they'll fit very well. Kate's at least a foot shorter than I am. And she doesn't have to stuff socks.

JON. Oh yeah? How do you know?

LESLIE. Because there are no sock marks on her clothes.

JON. Just try them on. I'll see if they fit or not. Sock marks.

LESLIE. (*Sulks towards the bedrooms.*) If I'm going to dress like a woman, I'd at least like to dress like a woman whose clothes fit. (*The TELEPHONE rings as* LESLIE *exits.* JON *rushes to it.*)

JON. Hello? Hi Connie. Yes, he's here. (*Calls.*) Leslie! Your girlfriend's on the phone.

LESLIE. (*Dashes back in with a look of terror.*) Who?

JON. (*Holds the uncovered phone towards him.*) Connie! Remember her?

LESLIE. Oh, her. Tell her I'm not home!

JON. (*Quickly covers the phone.*) I don't have to. You already did. What's going on between you two?

LESLIE. I'm breaking up with her and I'm trying to avoid it.

JON. (*Into phone.*) Connie? Now, stop crying. Here he is. He just came in. (*To* LESLIE.) Over the telephone is inhuman. (LESLIE *reluctantly takes the receiver.* JON *inspects the room. Decorates it throughout the scene.*)

LESLIE. Hi Connie, what's new? Now don't call me that. All right. I know. I know. You're right. I am that. Yes, I'm that too. Wait a minute. I'm not that. Connie, there's a good reason why I haven't called you. What is that reason? Well . . . (LESLIE *notices* JON *listening. To* JON.) You're right. Over the phone is pretty rotten. (*Into phone.*) It's not another woman. If there's one thing it's not it's another woman. There is no woman in my life at all.

JON. Tacky! Tacky! In person, Leslie! (JON *wanders out of hearing range.*)

LESLIE. Look Connie, there is a reason I haven't been seeing you . . . (JON *walks through.*) I just can't find the words right now. I've gone through a change. (JON *walks out.*) It's different than I've ever felt about a woman before. (JON *walks back in adding a last minute touch to the room.*) Look. Let's discuss this in person. Sure today is fine. See you later, goodbye. (*He hangs up the phone and instantly tries to salvage the connection.*) No, today is not fine. Hello? Hello? (*Hangs up.*) Nuts!

JON. Call her back!

LESLIE. I can't call her back.

JON. Why can't you call her back?

LESLIE. She was calling from a phone booth.

JON. How do you know?

LESLIE. The operator was calling me names.

JON. Great. What is Mr. Spinner going to say when the girl my wife used to date walks in?

LESLIE. Maybe he'll be gone by then.

JON. He better be. You're breaking up with Connie?

LESLIE. Yup. Breaking up with Connie.

JON. What for?

LESLIE. (*Makes noises.*) I've been thinking about it for years.

JON. You've only been seeing each other for about five months.

LESLIE. I know. But for years I always thought about breaking up with somebody.

JON. Leslie, you're not acting like yourself. I think the strain of today is too much for you to handle. Let's go over a few things. First of all, say nothing unless I ask you to speak. Got it?

LESLIE. I say nothing unless you ask me to speak. Got it.

JON. Remember to cross you legs like a girl.

LESLIE. What do you think? I'm gonna give this guy a cheap thrill? I know.

JON. And when all else fails, just smile. Let me see you smile. (LESLIE *makes a pained grin.*) Beautiful. If I wasn't married to you I'd marry you. You got all that?

LESLIE. That's it? That's all there is to being female? Smiling and crossing my legs?

JON. All you'll need to demonstrate today, yes.

LESLIE. I'm getting dressed. You've got an hour and forty-two minutes to get the place ready.

JON. Kate brought over a lot of stuff, didn't she?

LESLIE. Yes. She brought over some of her clothes and eight dollars of Salvation Army stuff.

JON. Then if you don't want to wear her clothes, wear the Salvation Army clothes!

LESLIE. I don't know where they've been. A diseased person could've worn them.

JON. Just get dressed Leslie! (LESLIE *exits to the bedrooms.* JON *surveys the room for a final inspection.*) Something's wrong. What's missing? What is it? (*Sniffs.*) It smells like Old Spice. Leslie! Wash your face! (JON *picks up a bottle of perfume and daintily sprays the room. Unsatisfied, he unscrews the top and pours the bottle along the top of the couch.*) A little Jungle Gardenia should do the trick. (*The DOORBELL rings. Glancing watch.*) Eleven-thirty. Leslie! Katie's back to help you get dressed. Come out and model a couple of things, will you?

LESLIE. (*Off.*) I'll be down in a minute, dear.

(JON *answers the door. It is not* KATE *as expected, but a proper middle-aged man. It is* FLOYD SPINNER. *He wears a suit and hat. He carries a briefcase. He wears glasses.* JON, *frozen, looks to the bedrooms, back to* SPINNER *and slams the door shut. The DOORBELL rings.* JON, *still in shock, opens the door.* FLOYD's *foot quickly gets into position for another door slam. His cigarette and hat are smashed into his face.*)

JON. Who are you?

FLOYD. Try, hello who are you. I'm Floyd Spinner, from the Internal Revenue Service. And I don't like having doors slammed in my face. You must be Jon Trachtman?

JON. Yes. What do you want?

FLOYD. I have an appointment. May I come in?

JON. (*Glancing towards the bedrooms.*) I guess so. Can I take your glasses? Er, your hat, I mean. Can I take your hat?

FLOYD. (*Hands over his hat and straightens his hair.*) Yes. Thank you.

JON. My but you're early. (JON *holds the hat under* SPINNER's *face and smacks his back in an effort to knock his glasses off.*) About two hours early.

FLOYD. I make it a practice to come early to catch people off-guard, hiding their cadillacs and swimming pools.

JON. (*Hands back* SPINNER's *hat when his efforts fail.*) We haven't got any swimming pool!

FLOYD. Figure of speech. Mrs. Trachtman, where is she?

JON. Back in Chicago.

FLOYD. Chicago? You said she'd be here.

JON. Oh. I thought you meant my mother. (*Laughs.*) Leslie goes around by her maiden name.

FLOYD. Yes. There's a lot of that going around now. I deplore it. When I married my wife, she changed her name to mine. That's the price of marriage, as far as I'm concerned.

JON. I can appreciate that, Mr. Spinner. Can I take your hat?

FLOYD. (*Handing it back again.*) Yes! Thank you! May I sit down?

JON. Of course. Forgive me. (JON *puts his hand on* FLOYD's *back to guide him.* SPINNER *leaps away.*)

FLOYD. I can see where the couch is. (FLOYD *sits. After a beat he recoils from the aroma.*)

JON. Something wrong, Mr. Spinner?

FLOYD. Not at all. I do hope the garbage strike ends soon.

JON. So do I. Would you like a drink?

FLOYD. No thank you.

JON. Well I would.

FLOYD. Fine. I'll just organize myself here. (JON *quickly retrieves a small drink from the bar.*)

FLOYD. When do I get to meet Mrs. Trachtman?

JON. Who? Oh. I'll go get her. Excuse me. (JON *heads for the bedrooms to warn* LESLIE. *But before he has taken one step,* LESLIE *enters—unannounced. He poses for* "KATE" *and* JON. *He is simply horrible to look at. He wears a bright red wig with a scarf tied over it. A big flowered bathrobe flows freely and fuzzy slippers cover his feet. His make-up has not been added yet. His face is*

covered solely with the clown-white base he applied earlier.
FLOYD, *preoccupied with his papers does not notice.* JON
gulps down his drink and introduces LESLIE, *who freezes at
the mention of* SPINNER'S *name.*) Mr. Spinner, I'd like you
to meet my wife.

FLOYD. (*Rises, smiling. He turns to greet* LESLIE *and
grimaces in horror at the sight.*) How do you do?

LESLIE. (*From bass to falsetto to a woman's voice.*)
Hello. Hello. Hellooo.

JON. Leslie just woke up. Forgive her for the way she's
dressed.

LESLIE. Forgive me.

FLOYD. Certainly. My wife doesn't look very good when
she gets up either. I'm sure that when you're all made up
and dressed you're a real beauty.

LESLIE. You'd be surprised.

JON. Shall we be seated?

(FLOYD *sits.* LESLIE *tries to run away but* JON *throws him
into the end chair.* JON *takes his seat. As* FLOYD
arranges his papers, JON *motions for* LESLIE *to cross
his legs. He tries and can't quite make it. With a little
work with his arms and a minute amount of pain,*
LESLIE *forces his legs into position. A look of agony
sweeps over his face just as* FLOYD *turns to ask him a
question.* FLOYD *decides against it and turns to* JON.)

FLOYD. I guess you're wondering why I'm here.

JON. Yes. We were. Weren't we dear?

LESLIE. (*In pain.*) Mm-hm.

FLOYD. Well. It seems to me that we have in our files the
fact that your wife Leslie is a man. Was a man.

JON. What can you mean? You mean like in a previous
life?

FLOYD. I mean like in a previous year. Mrs. Trachtman,
in the two years prior to your marriage, you filed your tax

returns as a man. Instead of marking female, you marked male. Why did you do that?

LESLIE. (*Quickly thinking.*) Yes, well, I figured that M stood for mother and F stood for father.

FLOYD. I'll buy that. M for mother and F for father. Mm-hm. Understandable, I suppose. M for mother. Yes. (FLOYD *writes vigorously in his report while* JON *shoots* LESLIE *a look as if he's just said the stupidest possible thing.* LESLIE *shrugs back.*)

JON. Leslie, dear, why don't you go get dressed and doll yourself up. I'll entertain Mr. Spinner for a while. (LESLIE *nods and rises. So does* FLOYD.) Oh. Are you leaving Mr. Spinner?

FLOYD. No. I'm being a gentleman.

JON. (*rising.*) Forgive me. We have a very informal house here. I tend to forget my manners. Hurry back dear. And put on some of your new perfume. What you're wearing now smells like a man's cologne.

FLOYD. Mr. Trachtman. That's a little harsh.

JON. Yes, well, we have a very harsh house here too.

FLOYD. I see.

JON. Go put on a dress dear.

LESLIE. I do have a smart pants suit I'd rather wear.

JON. I'd prefer a dress if you don't mind.

LESLIE. Well, I mind, but I'm in no position to argue. I won't be long, Mr. Spinner.

FLOYD. That's all right. Take your time. (LESLIE *is gone.*) Lovely woman. Lovely woman. Kind of reminds me of my wife.

JON. Really? How long have you been married?

FLOYD. Thirty-two years!

JON. Gee. Mr. Spinner, I'm sorry.

FLOYD. You're sorry? Now. May I see your wife's social security card and birth certificate?

JON. Certainly. Certainly. Here's his . . . here's historical proof. HER birth certificate.

FLOYD. Social security card?

JON. Right here.

FLOYD. Fine. Just give me a second. (FLOYD *writes in his report*. JON *grins, very sure of himself.*)

JON. That's all there is to it?

FLOYD. Yes. Your book-keeping isn't the subject of this investigation.

JON. Then you're finished?

FLOYD. I think so.

JON. Are you sure there isn't anything else you need?

FLOYD. Just one.

JON. What's that?

FLOYD. A Scotch on the rocks. I have to go home soon.

JON. Have to go home soon? Gee. That's too bad. Leslie and I were hoping you'd stay for dinner.

FLOYD. Oh. No thank you. I couldn't. I must get home.

JON. Then I guess you'd better. Your wife's probably waiting for you with open arms.

FLOYD. Yes, she probably is.

JON. Probably has a good meal cooked.

FLOYD. Could be. Could be.

JON. A little candle-lit dinner for two.

FLOYD. You think so?

JON. Yes. She probably has an intimate evening all planned for you when you get home.

FLOYD. I'll stay.

JON. How's that?

FLOYD. I'll stay for dinner.

JON. What for?

FLOYD. *You* spend an intimate evening with my wife. I'd rather stay here.

JON. But don't you think . . .

FLOYD. Usually people aren't this cordial with me. In fact, the last man I audited stapled a tea bag to the seat of my pants. Some people think they're so original. That was a Scotch on the rocks, please.

JON. Scotch on the rocks. Right.

(FLOYD *completes his report. JON pours a very tall glass of Scotch and drops in a tiny piece of ice. As he hands it to* FLOYD, LESLIE *sweeps into the room. He's changed from the robe into a screaming yellow chiffon dress. It is obviously much too small. He wears bright red tights and black high heels. The same red wig covers his head, but atop the clown-white base, bright red lipstick and blue eye shadow have been added. A mole has been drawn on his mouth like Joan Blondell. He stumbles in on the heels.*)

LESLIE. Sorry I took so long. I had a helluva time hooking my bra. (FLOYD *and* JON *react to the new outfit.*)
FLOYD. O my! Omigod. (LESLIE *stumbles.*) Are you all right?
JON. Leslie has bunyans. Nothing to worry about. (LESLIE *falls into the chair.*)
FLOYD. Your dress.
LESLIE. My dress?
FLOYD. It's so small.
LESLIE. It's that new washing machine. I told you I thought it was shrinking my clothes, Jon.
JON. Yeah. I'll have to take a look at it.
LESLIE. Let's look at it now before they get any smaller. Weren't you just leaving, Mr. Spinner?
JON. No. Mr. Spinner has agreed to stay for dinner Leslie. Isn't that great?
LESLIE. What?
JON. Yes. At first he wasn't going to but I talked him into it.
LESLIE. Well good for you.
FLOYD. What are you making, if I may ask?
LESLIE. (*Wide-eyed.*) I'm unemployed.

FLOYD. No. What are you making for dinner?

LESLIE. Oh. I thought you needed that for your report. (*Laughs.*)

(*Everyone politely laughs during which* LESLIE *frantically skims a McCall's Magazine looking for a meal.*)

FLOYD. No. No. I'll just need a few forms signed and the entire mess will be cleared up.

LESLIE. Mung Chowder Gumbo.

FLOYD. Beg pardon?

LESLIE. I'm making Mung Chowder Gumbo.

JON. Mung Chowder Gumbo?

FLOYD. Oh, really? I love that. I've always wanted to learn how to prepare it. May I watch you in the kitchen?

LESLIE. No you can't. It's my secret recipe.

FLOYD. But I won't squeal it.

LESLIE. I couldn't tell you. Really.

JON. Leslie's very old fashioned, Mr. Spinner. Here's your drink.

FLOYD. But I'm not through with this one.

JON. Then you'd better hurry. (FLOYD *gulps down his drink as* JON *hands him his second.*)

FLOYD. Before I go on being social like this, why don't I have you sign the forms, Mrs. Trachtman? (*The DOORBELL rings.*)

JON. Ah . . . why don't you go sign them in the kitchen?

FLOYD. The kitchen? What on earth for?

JON. The light's better in there.

FLOYD. I can see fine right in here.

JON. You can. Sure. But Leslie's eyes have been straining too much and the doctor said she'd go blind if she didn't sign things in the kitchen.

LESLIE. What are you talking . . .

(*Unseen by* FLOYD, JON *swats* LESLIE *in the face with a feather duster.* LESLIE *rubs his eyes and reacts.*)

JON. Look at her. She's straining them already.
FLOYD. My goodness. (*The DOORBELL rings.*) Just let me gather up my things. (*The DOORBELL rings.*) Aren't you going to answer that?
JON. Answer what? (*The DOORBELL rings.*)
FLOYD. That. The door. Aren't you going to answer the door?
JON. No I'm not. This building is flooded with Jehovah's Witnesses.
FLOYD. Jehovah's Witnesses?
LESLIE. Yes. Go away out there. We have all the cookies we want! (LESLIE *drags* FLOYD *to the kitchen.*)
JON. Here, don't forget your drink.

(FLOYD *takes his drink and* LESLIE *drags him off.* JON *quickly answers the door. It is* KATE, *dressed beautifully. A nice contrast to make* LESLIE *look worse.*)

KATE. Who's selling cookies? I'm sorry I'm late, but the bus got a flat tire on 31st Street and I had to walk.
JON. Kate . . .
KATE. We haven't got much time. Give me a kiss hello.
JON. But Leslie . . .
KATE. Leslie would want it this way. (KATE *grabs him and kisses him passionately.* FLOYD *enters unnoticed.*)
FLOYD. Oh excuse me. I forgot my pen. (JON *and* KATE *freeze.* FLOYD *gets his pen and crosses back to kitchen. He does a double-take.*) Boy, all they give me is pamphlets.
JON. There's a good reason for this.
FLOYD. There always is. No need to explain. I was surprised to think you'd be content being married to . . . she's a nice lady and all that . . . but . . . how shall I put it? Woof. Woof.

KATE. Woof. Woof? Who is this man?

JON. Mr. Spinner from the I.R.S. . . Kate my friend.

KATE. How do you do. You're early.

JON. He came to look at our swimming pool.

FLOYD. Dear, Mrs. Trachtman is in the kitchen.

KATE. Your mother's here?

FLOYD. No, she's in Chicago. I mean Leslie, his wife.

JON. Yeah Kate, you'd better beat it before she finds you here.

LESLIE. (*Sweeps in, now enjoying himself.*) Mr. Spinner! Where did you run off to, you naughty boy!

KATE. Leslie?

LESLIE. Oh. Hello Kate dearie.

FLOYD. You two know each other?

LESLIE. Of course we do. Kate and I are sisters.

JON. That's right. Kate is Leslie's sister.

LESLIE. Don't you notice the resemblance?

FLOYD. It's uncanny.

KATE. Yes. If you'll excuse me, I'll bring these dresses up to Leslie's room.

FLOYD. Oh those are Leslie's dresses?

LESLIE. Oh yes. We wear the same size. So we mix and match with each other all the time. Isn't that right Sis?

KATE. (*Glaring.*) Yes, that's right. Excuse me. (KATE *exits to the bedroom.*)

FLOYD. Wow. What a set-up.

LESLIE. I beg your pardon? What do you mean?

FLOYD. You and your sister can share clothes. I imagine that must cut down on your expenses. (FLOYD *winks at* JON.)

JON. You two had better get back to signing your forms. If you'd like, I'll get out of your way by joining Kate upstairs.

LESLIE. No. We'll go to the kitchen. My eyes, remember?

FLOYD. We wouldn't want Mrs. Trachtman to go blind.

LESLIE. That's right, we wouldn't want that. (*Takes pen.*)
I'll go put my Joan Hancock on your papers. (LESLIE *exits
with a flourish.*)

FLOYD. You rascal. You rascal! What a set-up. How do
you do it?

JON. It just happened.

FLOYD. When did it all start?

JON. What time is it?

FLOYD. Oh look. My drink is empty. May I get a refill?

JON. Allow me. (JON *pours another tall glass of Scotch.
This time no ice.*)

FLOYD. That Kate is one cutie. Why didn't you marry
her? Why did you marry Leslie?

JON. I kind of had to.

FLOYD. Is that so? I don't recall any children. My report
would have mentioned something.

JON. Oh that's right. I meant that I had to because of
Leslie's father. The Colonel. Shotgun, you see.

FLOYD. A shotgun wedding? That's horrible.

JON. Well you learn to live with it. Please don't mention
it in front of Leslie. She gets hysterical.

FLOYD. I understand (*The DOORBELL rings.*)

JON. Oh no.

FLOYD. What is it? One of those damn peddlers again?

JON. Yes, let's just ignore it.

FLOYD. You can't let them rule you. I'll handle it.
(*Yells.*) Beat it, creep! Or I'll have the manager throw you
out. (*To* JON.) Well, I'd better get back to your wife.

(FLOYD *proudly exits to the kitchen.* JON *composes himself
and answers the door. In storms* VIVIAN TRACHTMAN;
*a middle-aged stoic woman in a smart outfit and a
bubble-cut blonde hairdo. She carries two suitcases
and is very out of breath.*)

JON. Mom!

VIVIAN. Who are you calling a creep? (VIVIAN *storms to the couch and kicks off her shoes. She glances around. It is evidently her first trip here.*)

JON. What are you doing here?

VIVIAN. That's a helluva greeting. I take it you never got my telegram. I stood around that La Guardia airport for three hours. Oh, that place was filthy. I refused to sit down. I wouldn't go near the woman's room, even though I was bursting. My feet are aching. My head is throbbing. Oh! And to complete my morning, a man exposed himself to me in the baggage claim.

JON. What telegram?

VIVIAN. Is that all you heard me say? I said a man exposed himself to your mother in the baggage claim. I hit him with my shoe. Right where it counts too. I left him rolling around on the conveyor belt. I hobbled out to the curb and hailed a cab, which was no easy task, and here I am.

JON. Here you are.

VIVIAN. My head is throbbing. Do you have any aspirin?

JON. You know what's good for a headache, mom? A walk. A nice long walk.

VIVIAN. I don't want to go for a walk. What's wrong with you? You could at least act pleased and give me a kiss hello. You haven't seen me in months.

JON. (*Kissing her.*) I'm sorry mom. What are you doing here?

VIVIAN. I explained it all in my telegram. I came to help you with the wedding arrangements. I want to make this special for you dear.

JON. Thanks mom. Why don't you start with the caterer and when you get back we can talk.

VIVIAN. We can talk now. I'll take care of all that later. Your letter said nothing. You told me you were getting married and you told me the date. And that's all you told me. I don't even know the girl's name!

JON. Yeah well. We decided in kind of a hurry.

VIVIAN. She's not pregnant, is she?

JON. No. We just felt it was about time. As soon as we decided, I mailed you out that letter. That was only four days ago!

VIVIAN. I know. And five minutes after I read it, I packed, wired out that telegram and here I am.   •

JON. What telegram? Leslie never said anything about any telegram.

VIVIAN. Leslie? You know, I've never met the dear. I can't believe you've roomed together for more than four years and we've never met. I can't wait to see his face when we finally meet.

JON. I can't wait to see yours.

VIVIAN. I miss you Jon. Holidays are too far apart. Give me a hug. (JON *and* VIVIAN *hug each other.* JON, *facing the kitchen.* FLOYD *enters.*)

FLOYD. Omigod, another one.

VIVIAN. I beg your pardon. Another what? Who are you? Who is that?

JON. Mom. I'd like you to meet Mr. Spinner from the Internal Revenue Service. Mr. Spinner, I'd like you to meet my mother, Vivian Trachtman.

FLOYD. How do you do?

VIVIAN. The Internal Revenue Service?

FLOYD. Yes. There was a mix-up on their tax return, Leslie's and your son's. But we're all straightened out now.

VIVIAN. Thank heavens. Where is Leslie? I've never met the dear.

FLOYD. You've never met?

VIVIAN. No. I live in Chicago and I've barely even seen Jon for the past four years. He's talked about Leslie though. And now, at last, we'll meet.

JON. No. I don't know if that's such a hot idea.

FLOYD. Don't be nervous. She's not much on looks, but she's a very nice lady.

VIVIAN. I beg your pardon?

FLOYD. Perhaps that was a little harsh, but they run a harsh house here. Right Mr. Trachtman?

JON. That's right.

FLOYD. I'll be right back. (FLOYD *rushes out to the kitchen.*)

VIVIAN. What did he mean, I'm not much on looks? I think I do all right.

JON. Look, mom, I haven't got much time to explain.

VIVIAN. It doesn't matter dear. You know, this apartment isn't as bad as I thought it would be.

JON. I know, mom, I haven't got much time to explain but . . .

VIVIAN. Amazing what you can find at garage sales these days.

JON. . . . Mr. Spinner thinks we're married and we're not . . .

VIVIAN. Dimmer lighting would hide the stains on the couch, Jon.

JON. . . . He thinks Leslie and I are married and of course we're not.

VIVIAN. If you'd like, I'll redo the whole apartment while I'm here.

JON. Listen to me, mom. Just pretend that Leslie and I are married in front of Mr. Spinner, all right?

VIVIAN. What are you saying dear?

JON. Look. I saved us money by pretending that Leslie and I are married.

VIVIAN. I don't think I understand. But I'll do whatever you want. That's what I'm here for.

KATE. (*Sneaks down the stairs.*) Is he gone yet?

JON. Kate!

KATE. You must be Mrs. Spinner. I'm Leslie's sister, Kate.

VIVIAN. How do you do. I didn't know Leslie had a sister.

JON. Kate.

KATE. Oh yes. In fact, Leslie picked out this dress for me to wear.

VIVIAN. Isn't that nice.

JON. Kate, this is my mother.

KATE. Your what?

FLOYD. (*Rushes in, the bearer of good news.*) Get ready Mrs. Trachtman. Leslie! There's someone out here just dying to meet you!

LESLIE. (*Sweeps into the room, now donning an apron over his dress, waving a handkerchief.*) Charmed. Simply charmed, my dear.

VIVIAN. Omigod.

(VIVIAN *collapses in a faint.* FLOYD *rushes to her aid.* JON *smacks* LESLIE. KATE'S *mouth drops open. All as the curtain comes down.*)

ACT TWO

AT RISE we find it is but a few moments later. VIVIAN *is still unconscious on the couch.* FLOYD, *at her side.* LESLIE *is pacing upstage.* KATE *is Off-Right, in the kitchen.* JON, *at his mother's side, slaps her wrists.*

JON. Gosh. She's out cold.

FLOYD. Mrs. Trachtman. Wake up. Wake up. Maybe she's dead. Are you dead, Mrs. Trachtman?

JON. Kate! Did you find any smelling salts?

KATE. (*Enters from the kitchen with a huge chunk of cheese. She crosses to* VIVIAN *with it.*) This is the best I could do. Limburger cheese.

LESLIE. Oh. That'll wake up anything.

FLOYD. (*Takes the cheese and waves it under* VIVIAN'S *nose. She starts to groggily come around.*) Mrs. Trachtman. Wake up!

LESLIE. (*To* JON.) You better get us out of this, buster.

VIVIAN. What? What? Jon! Help. Oh, God. He's stuffing cheese up my nose. Jon!

JON. Mom, relax. You fainted.

VIVIAN. Oh, I . . . Get that away from me! (FLOYD *rests the cheese down and pours a glass of Bourbon, which he tries to hand to a resisting* VIVIAN. KATE *exits to kitchen with the cheese.*)

FLOYD. Here. Take a sip of this.

VIVIAN. No.

FLOYD. It'll calm you down.

VIVIAN. Oh, no. I never drink. No.

FLOYD. Just a sip. Come on.

VIVIAN. (*Gulps down the shot. She hands back the glass for a refill.*) Thank you.

LESLIE. You shouldn't drink it so fast, mom. It'll rot your guts out.

VIVIAN. You! How dare you call me mom. Oh, what a dirty trick you two have played on me. I'm so disappointed in you, son. After all I've taught you. If your father was alive, he'd die of shame.

FLOYD. Now, now. Looks aren't everything.

VIVIAN. I raised my son with certain ideals. I never thought he'd end up like this. With that.

LESLIE. It's not as bad as it looks, mom.

FLOYD. Yes. She could try attending Barbizon.

VIVIAN. What the hell is this man talking about?

FLOYD. Mrs. Trachtman, you're too wound up. Here, have another sip of this.

VIVIAN. No, I . . . thank you. (VIVIAN *takes the glass and the bottle. She continues downing refills throughout the scene.* KATE *re-enters wiping hands with a towel.*) This is an embarrassment to the entire family. One total embarrassment.

JON. Mom, you don't understand.

VIVIAN. I don't understand? I understand perfectly. You lied to me. He lied to me, Mr. Spinner. I expected a different kind of Leslie. Certainly not this.

FLOYD. That's what I thought. But I'm sure Jon stretched the truth to keep from hurting you.

VIVIAN. Hurting me? This is going to kill me.

FLOYD. My wife looks just like Leslie and it doesn't bother me a bit.

VIVIAN. What the hell does your wife have to do with any of this?

JON. Mom, I think you've had enough to drink.

VIVIAN. Look. Look who's telling me to stop drinking. My son the liar. I'll drink as much as I damn well please. (*To prove her point,* VIVIAN *chugs half the bottle. Everyone stands by helpless.*)

LESLIE. Easy does it, mom.

VIVIAN. Stop calling me mom!

KATE. Do something, Jon.

JON. Leslie, let me talk to my mother before she blows the whole thing.

LESLIE. Good idea. I'll go upstairs and powder my nose before I get a shiner. Nice meeting you, mom. (LESLIE *exits to the bedrooms.* VIVIAN *and* FLOYD *are downing the entire bottle dry.*)

JON. Mr. Spinner! She's calm enough! I need to speak with my mother. Alone.

FLOYD. I'll go wait in the kitchen. (FLOYD *ambles out to the kitchen.*)

JON. Mom, please put the bottle down.

VIVIAN. I ought to break it and slit my wrists with it. (FLOYD *is gone.*)

VIVIAN. How can you do this to me? How can the two of you live together? How can you do this with a girl you aren't even married to?

JON. Mom, you've got it all wrong.

FLOYD. (*Re-enters.*) Excuse me. I forgot my drink. (FLOYD *retrieves his drink as* VIVIAN *continues her tirade.*)

VIVIAN. Come on. After all these years you can't say you've never been to bed with her.

JON. (*Aware of* FLOYD.) You don't understand. Leslie's not like other girls.

FLOYD. Yes, Mrs. Trachtman. It's not easy for Jon. It wasn't easy for me either. It took me seven years and I still make my wife put a bag over her head.

KATE. Jon, you're not handling this very well. Take Mr. Spinner in the kitchen. I'll speak to your mother.

JON. All right. Mr. Spinner, do you mind?

FLOYD. I want to stay here and hear this. (JON *almost shoves* FLOYD *off into the kitchen.* KATE, *now alone, braves herself and confronts Mrs. Trachtman.*)

KATE. Mrs. Trachtman, please listen to me.

VIVIAN. You said your name was Kate, didn't you?

KATE. That's right.

VIVIAN. Well, Jon used to talk about a Kate. That was

you, wasn't it? When he said he was going to get married, I assumed he was going to marry you.

KATE. Well, he was. Until Leslie came along and I . . .

VIVIAN. I know. I know. You don't have to tell me the rest.

KATE. Yes I do. You see, Jon and I have been dating for about a year now . . .

VIVIAN. Even though he's living with Leslie?

KATE. Well, yes.

VIVIAN. You condone his living with Leslie?

KATE. Sure I do. That started back in college.

VIVIAN. Didn't you say that Leslie was your sister?

KATE. Yes I did, but . . .

VIVIAN. Omigod. This is incest, isn't it?

KATE. No. No it's . . .

VIVIAN. My heart. My heart is going to stop beating.

KATE. Mrs. Trachtman, you don't know what you're talking about.

VIVIAN. Are you calling me an idiot?

KATE. You're putting words in my mouth.

VIVIAN. First, your family corrupts my son and now you're calling me names. You slut! (*The DOORBELL rings.*)

KATE. I don't think I'm handling this very well.

VIVIAN. (*Hiccups.*) Excuse me.

KATE. I'll get it. Don't try to get up. Just lay there.

JON. (*Enters from the kitchen. He calls back in after him.*) Mr. Spinner, don't put that on your head. I'll be right back. (*To KATE.*) Everything straightened out?

KATE. Well . . . sort of.

JON. Good. (JON *opens the door. In walks* JANSEN *wearing a catcher's mask.*)

JANSEN. Afternoon, Jon. Carmen. Oh? Got company?

JON. Yes, Mr. Jansen. My mother's here.

JANSEN. I know. I read the telegram.

JON. What telegram?

JANSEN. Why's she smelling the couch?

KATE. She's resting. She's tired from her plane ride.

JANSEN. I know how it is. I took a plane once.

JON. I'm glad for you, Mr. Jansen, and now why don't you go take a hike.

JANSEN. To Boston. Because of a blizzard or a tornado or something it took an extra half an hour to land. Boy!

KATE. Tiring?

JANSEN. No. I threw my guts up.

FLOYD. (*Swaggers in.*) It's lonely in there. Hello, I'm Floyd Spinner. (FLOYD *extends his hand.* JANSEN *ignores it.*)

JANSEN. Relative?

JON. No.

JANSEN. Good. Looks like a tax collector.

KATE. Why don't you help yourself to a beer in the refrigerator?

JANSEN. Don't mind if I do. (JANSEN *exits into the kitchen.* FLOYD *follows.*)

FLOYD. I'll show you where it is. (FLOYD *exits with him.*)

KATE. Jon. Hide all the things I brought over and get him out of here. You know how he is. If he thinks there's a girl living here, you're sunk!

JON. Omigod. Leslie!

LESLIE. (*Skips in.*) Everything cleared up? Oh, I see mom's been playing chug-a-lug again.

JON. She's asleep, knock it off! Take all of Kate's things and hide them upstairs. Jansen's in the kitchen.

LESLIE. Can I get undressed?

JON. No, Spinner might see you. Just hide up there. When he's gone I'll come get you.

LESLIE. I'm getting tired of playing house, Jon!

JON. As soon as I can get rid of Jansen, we'll feed Spinner and throw him out. It won't be much longer.

LESLIE. It better not be. I'm going to need a shave soon.

JON. I hope you can cook.

LESLIE. All I was supposed to do was smile and cross my legs, remember?

KATE. Will the two of you stop talking and clean this place up?!

(JON, LESLIE *and* KATE *frantically collect up a bra, a bathing suit, 2 hats, a mink stole, 2 pocketbooks, a pair of stockings, the lace tablecloth and the scatter rug.* FLOYD *enters from the kitchen.*

FLOYD. That man is slipping beer cans into his pockets. What are you doing?

LESLIE. It's almost dinner-time. I have to straighten up the apartment.

FLOYD. Anything you'd like me to do?

LESLIE. Aside from going home, I can't think of a thing.

FLOYD. Fine. Then I'll just keep Mrs. Trachtman company.

KATE. Yes. You do that.

FLOYD. I hope you're feeling better, Mrs. Trachtman.

VIVIAN. (*With a start.*) What?

FLOYD. You're looking a little better.

VIVIAN. If you comment on my looks one more time, I'll hit you with my shoe.

FLOYD. Look at them cleaning up. You're certainly in a hurry!

LESLIE. Oh yes. We can't tell you how quickly we'd like this all to be over.

(JANSEN *backs in from the kitchen. He is still wearing the catcher's mask. From the bulges in his clothes, it is apparent that he's stolen some of their beer. He guzzles one open can.* JON *spies him and throws* LESLIE *and* KATE *upstairs with all the clothes. A BATHING CAP and A BLUE SASH remain behind. As* JANSEN *turns around,* JON *spies them and s*   *   in his clothes.*)

JANSEN. Sorry. I took your last can.

JON. Mr. Jansen, what brought you up here?

JANSEN. Oh yeah. I wanted to return Leslie's mask. (JANSEN *removes the mask and hands it to* JON, *as* FLOYD *turns around eavesdropping.*)

FLOYD. Leslie's what?

JANSEN. Mask. Mask. What are you deaf?

FLOYD. No sir, I'm just a little blind. Why would Leslie need a mask like that?

JANSEN. Oh, Leslie doesn't like to wear it. But Jon can get pretty forceful.

FLOYD. Mr. Trachtman, when does Leslie wear that thing?

JON. Well, actually . . .

JANSEN. When they're playing, when do you think?

FLOYD. I don't understand. Playing?

JON. (*Winking.*) Yes, Mr. Spinner. Playing. Like you play with your wife.

FLOYD. Oh. Playing. Oh! Doesn't that make things awkward?

JANSEN. Naw. It's kind of hard to talk, but what do you need words for? Am I right, Jon?

JON. Well, I . . .

JANSEN. Besides, I wouldn't want my teeth bashed in.

FLOYD. Teeth bashed in?

JANSEN. Why are you so surprised? You never know where it's going to go. One good pop to the mouth and you could break your nose.

FLOYD. I must be reading the wrong books.

JANSEN. What's so hard to understand? Some people play so rough you end up with spikes driven through your face.

FLOYD (T N.) Well, no wonder you and Leslie don't sleep togeth :

JANSEN. (*Laughs.*) That's a good one. (*Notices* VIVIAN.) Hey what's wrong with your mother?

Nothing. She's just a little upset.

EN. She looks a little plastered.

FLOYD. She's upset about the little lady upstairs.

JANSEN. The what? You got a lady upstairs?

JON. He doesn't mean lady. He means Leslie.

JANSEN. Yeah, Four-eyes. Leslie is no lady.

VIVIAN. You can say that again.

JANSEN. Is there a woman upstairs?

KATE.(*Rushes in to block the entrance.*) Hi Mr. Jansen. How's it going?

JANSEN. You! You're living here!

VIVIAN. He knows about her too?

JON. She is not living here.

FLOYD. No one lives here but Leslie and Jon.

VIVIAN. Let's not advertise it, thank you.

JON. I swear. No one lives here but Leslie and me.

JANSEN. Just a second. I'm the manager of this building. And a certain Leslie Arthur gave me permission to search this apartment whenever I want to. And I want to now.

JON. Leslie gave you permission.

JANSEN. Yes. Candy was here when Leslie said so. Am I right, Candy?

KATE. Yes, but . . .

JANSEN. (*Picks her up and puts her down on the floor, out of his way.*) Pardone. (JANSEN *is up the steps in seconds and off.*)

JON. This is illegal!

JANSEN. (*Off.*) Then call the F.B.I.!

KATE. What do we do now?

JON. I'm gonna make him pay for those beers.

FLOYD. Why does he think all three of you live here?

VIVIAN. They might as well be.

JON. Mom please!

(*Everything grows quiet. Everyone looks upstairs. They hear silence. They sit on the couch in fear, KATE apart from the rest on an armchair. After another moment of silence, they shift positions and listen again. Silence. They shift positions again.*)

JON. You don't suppose he fell asleep.

FLOYD. Where is Leslie, anyway?

JON. Upstairs, I thought. (*They look Off* L. *for* LESLIE *and* JANSEN. *Behind them, unseen, we see* LESLIE—*still in drag—edging his way along the ledge, carrying all the dresses, props and knick-knacks.* KATE, *alone, spies him and rises in horror.*)

JON. Where could she be? What's happening up there? Maybe we should go look for her.

KATE. No! Don't move! (VIVIAN, FLOYD *and* JON *all freeze at her command.*)

JON. What?

KATE. Gee, the three of you together like that would make a great picture. Don't move. I'll go get my camera.

JON. Kate! Get your camera? I don't think this is the time.

FLOYD. Oh, I'd love to pose for a picture.

KATE. Goooood. Stay right there. Don't move a hair until I get back. (VIVIAN *and* FLOYD *pose and freeze as instructed.* JON *is confused.*)

JON. Kate. I'd rather find Leslie, if that's all right with you. (*Out on the ledge,* LESLIE *has lost his balance. All the clothes and props fall to the earth below,* LESLIE *regaining balance.*)

KATE. Oh. Oh. Ooooh! How high up are we?

JON. What?

KATE. What floor is this?

JON. The fifth. Why? Do you want to take a picture of the elevator now?

FLOYD. Fine with me. I don't care where we pose.

JON. Oh shut up. Do you mind if we go upstairs and look for Leslie? (LESLIE *falls off the ledge.*)

KATE. Leslie!!!

VIVIAN. Don't call for her, Kate. We'll look around ourselves. (FLOYD *and* JON *rise.*)

FLOYD. Where do you suppose she is right now, Kate?

KATE. Oh, you know Leslie. She's all over the place.

JON. What are you talking about?

KATE. I have to go now.

JON. Why are you leaving? I thought you could help us with dinner.

KATE. Yeah well. I have to go pick up a few things. (*Laughs.*)

JON. Would you please sit down. (JON *forces* KATE *down as* JANSEN *re-enters.*)

JANSEN. Nothing there.

JON. What do you mean, "nothing there?" Nothing's there?

JANSEN. No women's clothes and no women.

JON. What about a Leslie? Did you find a Leslie up there?

JANSEN. No. There's nothing up there.

JON. Then where the hell . . .

JANSEN. I gotta go. Nice meeting you, Mrs. Trachtman. You're my kind of woman. Drunk. Thanks for the brew. (JANSEN *exits out the front door.* KATE *pops up.*)

KATE. Jon, I have to talk to you.

JON. Kate, don't start with that camera stuff again. I want to see where Leslie went. (JON *rushes upstairs.* KATE *calls after him.*)

KATE. But Jon, I . . . Oh! (*The DOORBELL rings.*)

FLOYD. What a busy place.

KATE. Mrs. Trachtman's asleep again. Would you mind getting that cheese, Mr. Spinner? (FLOYD *crosses towards the kitchen. The DOORBELL rings.* JON *rushes back downstairs.*)

FLOYD. Shall I get that?

KATE. No! Go get the cheese. Get the cheese!

(KATE *pushes* FLOYD *off into the kitchen.* KATE *and* JON *exchange a look, then open the door. In stumbles* LESLIE; *wigless, scratched up and wearing a ripped dress. He can barely stand and wears one shoe.* JON *and* KATE *help support his sagging legs. He is out of breath.*)

JON. Where the hell have you been? Where's your wig? Are you trying to blow the whole thing?

KATE. I've been trying to tell you. He went out on the ledge when Jansen came in and he slipped off. I thought he was dead.

JON. Great. Now what are we supposed to do about your hair?

KATE. He just missed killing himself and all you care about is how his hair looks?

JON. If we get caught, we might as well be dead.

KATE. How can you be so heartless. Leslie, what broke your fall?

LESLIE. You haven't lived until you've skydived into Mrs. Gill, sunbathing on her terrace.

JON. You fell onto Mrs. Gill? I'm surprised you didn't bounce back up to the ledge.

KATE. You poor thing. Are you all right?

LESLIE. Yeah. The fall didn't bother me. But it's the first time I ever saw Mrs. Gill without her stretch pants on.

JON. What happened to your wig?

LESLIE. The last time I saw it, it was halfway down the throat of her German shepherd.

JON. What happened to your dress?

LESLIE. I tried to get the wig back.

KATE. Oh you poor thing.

JON. Wait a minute. Where's Spinner?

KATE. He's in the kitchen.

JON. Leslie, I still have a couple of Kate's things here. Maybe I can doctor you up. Kate, you distract him and we'll go get dressed.

KATE. How am I supposed to do that?

JON. The same way you distract me. You're a woman. He's a man. There's enough difference right there for some sort of distractment.

KATE. I can't do that.

JON. Yes you can. Leslie, don't you find Kate distracting?

LESLIE. Wgha . . . wflagh . . .

JON. Oh great. The fall must've knocked his sinuses loose. Come on, let's go get dressed.

(JON *and* LESLIE *run off into the bedroom.* KATE *turns around in time to see* FLOYD *enter with the cheese.*)

FLOYD. Here it is. (FLOYD *crosses towards the coffee table, but is stopped by* KATE.)

KATE. Mr. Spinner. I want to tell you how much I admire men that work for the Internal Revenue Service.

FLOYD. You do?

KATE. Oh yes. It's such a macho position. Out on the streets, risking your life every day. I didn't have the chance to tell you before.

FLOYD. If you'd like, I could have your return audited and you could tell me again.

KATE. Would you? You're my kind of man, Floyd.

FLOYD. Thank you. You're not bad yourself. I know how you younger girls are, these days. More open to having affairs with whoever you want to, whenever you want to, wherever you want to. And with all due respect to Mr. Trachtman . . . I'm all for it, baby! (*He begins chasing her around the room, unbuttoning his shirt.*)

KATE. Mr. Spinner! Is this any way for an I.R.S. man to act?

FLOYD. Oh yes. In the old days, a lot of people got out of paying taxes this way.

KATE. Mr. Spinner!

FLOYD. Don't fight it. It's kismet. It's kismet. Kiss me Kate . . .

KATE. No! What about Mrs. Trachtman?

FLOYD. I don't want to kiss her.

KATE. She's right there on the couch!

FLOYD. She's asleep. And evidently, Jon and Leslie have left us all alone.

(With a shove from the back, LESLIE enters. He's adorned in his regular drag clothes with an additional pink bathing cap, covering up his hair, and a big blue sash draped over most of the rips in the dress. JON is behind him, pushing.)

JON. Here she is, everybody!

FLOYD. Good God. What happened to you?

LESLIE. Mm?

FLOYD. What happened to your hair?

LESLIE. A dog ate it.

JON. What a kidder. She just took a shower. Leslie's always taking showers. Isn't that right, Leslie? She has a hygiene problem.

LESLIE. That does it. I'm getting undressed.

FLOYD. No. No. I'll take his word for it.

JON. You'd better start dinner, dear. Mr. Spinner has to get going soon.

LESLIE. And I have to do the cooking?

JON. That's right.

LESLIE. Pot luck tonight, folks. (LESLIE *crosses towards the kitchen.)*

FLOYD. May I help?

LESLIE. Sure. The more the merrier. Why don't you bring mom along too?

FLOYD. Mrs. Trachtman is still asleep.

VIVIAN. The hell I am. I just can't lift my eyelids up. *(The TELEPHONE rings.)*

VIVIAN. What's that?

KATE. The phone. I'll get it.

FLOYD. May I escort you to the kitchen, Mrs. Trachtman?

VIVIAN. As long as I can lean on you.

LESLIE. Why don't you two take out all the ingredients and I'll join you in a minute.

FLOYD. Which ingredients do you need?

LESLIE. You name it, I'll use it.

FLOYD. All right. This is going to be fun. Come along Mrs. Trachtman. (FLOYD *and* VIVIAN *hobble out to the kitchen.*)

VIVIAN. (*Exiting.*) I don't feel so good.

KATE. (*Hanging up phone.*) That was someone named Connie. She apologized for being late and said she'd be right over.

LESLIE. Excuse me.

KATE. Where are you going?

LESLIE. I'm jumping off the ledge again.

KATE. Why, who's Connie?

JON. That's Leslie's girlfriend.

KATE. Leslie's what?

JON. Girlfriend. Funny, how you've never met.

LESLIE. It's a scream, Jon.

KATE. Leslie's girlfriend?

LESLIE. Old girlfriend. It's over. We broke up.

JON. Not yet you didn't.

KATE. Yes, why don't you go jump off the ledge?!

LESLIE. I . . . flbagh . . . wait a minute. Ghalthh . . . I can explain.

JON. Explain what?

KATE. Nothing. There's nothing to explain. Leslie said it's over and I believe him. It's over.

LESLIE. Now Kate, hrrahh . . .

JON. What's all this fuss about Connie? You never even met her, Kate.

KATE. I know. But it doesn't matter. I didn't know Leslie was that misleading. Or that insensitive.

JON. That's what I told you, Leslie.

LESLIE. Wghallf . . . bflagh . . .

KATE. Oh, go blow your nose!

VIVIAN. (*Enters.*) Get in here, Leslie. I want to see you prepare this Mung Chowder Gumbo.

LESLIE. No. I don't want to.

VIVIAN. Look, Leslie, I already dislike you. Don't make me despise you.

JON. I guess you'd better go in there.

LESLIE. I don't feel like it.

VIVIAN. And she's rude too, Jon.

KATE. Get in there, Leslie, or I'll spill the beans.

LESLIE. Come on, mom. Let's go play chef. I'll be Julia Child and you can be Vincent Price. (VIVIAN *and* LESLIE *exit.*)

JON. Good hint, Kate. I didn't know you made Mung Chowder Gumbo with beans.

KATE. Yes. Mung beans. Jon, please forgive me. I'm so sorry.

JON. For what? This'll all be over soon. I'm the one who should apologize. I've been neglecting you these past few weeks. With all my trying to get our band jobs, I haven't had any time for you. When this is all over we can get back to normal. I'm sorry too.

KATE. I love you.

JON. I love you too, Moonpie.

(VIVIAN *enters from the kitchen on a bee-line upstairs for the bathroom to be ill in.*)

VIVIAN. You should see the mess in there. I'm going to be sick.

JON. Do you know where the bathroom is?

VIVIAN. At this point, it doesn't matter. (*She is gone.*)

JON. What's Leslie doing in there? What are we going to do? Leslie can't even defrost meat.

KATE. I don't know. We could sneak in some food.

JON. Good idea I'll go. You help Leslie bluff it until I get back. (JON *rushes out the front door.* FLOYD *enters from the kitchen.*)

FLOYD. Did you know Mung Chowder Gumbo is made with molasses and tuna fish? This is thrilling. Where's Mr. Trachtman? He's missing all of this.

KATE. He just went for a walk.

FLOYD. Did he? Then that makes us almost secluded, doesn't it?

KATE. He went for a short walk. Now, hold on. Mr. Spinner, you can think all you want to about me but I'm still not interested in having an affair with you. Think of your wife!

FLOYD. Yech!

KATE. Think of Jon! He'll kill you!

FLOYD. If he comes near me, I'll blab to your father about the two of you.

KATE. My father?

FLOYD. The Colonel. The shotgun expert.

KATE. (*Totally confused.*) Oh him? . . . He's off hunting somewhere.

FLOYD. Come here!

KATE. No! Think of his mother in the bathroom!

FLOYD. I beg your pardon?

KATE. Think of his mother!

FLOYD. Her interest is in her son and his wife. Not her son's mistress and the I.R.S. man.

KATE. Then think of . . . isn't there someone you should be thinking of?

FLOYD. No. Come here!

KATE. No! (KATE *backs into the table holding the empty breakaway Bourbon bottle. She picks it up and hides it behind her.*)

FLOYD. Give me a kiss.

KATE. No! (FLOYD *has* KATE *pinned against the table.*)

FLOYD. Come on. Give it to me, baby.

KATE. If you say so. (FLOYD *puckers up with his eyes closed.* KATE *knocks him unconscious. He falls onto her then onto the floor.* LESLIE *enters.*)

LESLIE. Mr. Spinner, it's time for the cream and vinegar. Mr. Spinner! Where is he?

KATE. Down there. I knocked him out.

LESLIE. You certainly have a way with men.

KATE. He tried to get me on the couch.

LESLIE. So what? Everybody else has.

KATE. Don't start, Leslie. Mrs. Trachtman will be down any minute. What should we do with him?

LESLIE. Give me a hand. We'll prop him up on the couch. (LESLIE *and* KATE *lift* FLOYD *onto the couch.*)

LESLIE. Here. Put this glass in his hand. Cross his legs. Here. Give him a cigarette. There. He's in a drunken stupor.

VIVIAN. (*Enters, still nauseous.* FLOYD *slips off the couch onto the floor.*) I feel so much better. Where's Jon?

LESLIE. He went for a walk.

VIVIAN. Where's Floyd?

LESLIE. He's right . . . in the kitchen. He's very excited about cooking dinner. Why don't you go help him. You can pour in the custard for me.

VIVIAN. Well, hurry up. I'm doing it all myself. (VIVIAN *exits and* LESLIE *and* KATE *lift* FLOYD *back onto the couch.* LESLIE *stuffs pillow under his legs to keep him in place.*)

LESLIE. There. That should hold him there.

KATE. Thank you. It's very nice of you to help me, considering you're a bastard!

LESLIE. What do you mean? I tried to explain before . . .

KATE. What's to explain? It's all right for me to tell Jon we're through. But you hadn't quite gotten around to telling Connie about us. If you had any intention of doing so at all.

LESLIE. Now Kate . . .

KATE. Oh, let's stop kidding ourselves, Leslie. This was a mistake from the beginning. The only reason we were attracted to each other in the first place was because of boredom.

LESLIE. Oh yeah? Listen, Moonpie . . .

KATE. Don't you ever call me Moonpie. Jon calls me Moonpie. Jon loves me. Jon wouldn't lie to me. Jon is open and honest.

LESLIE. Honest? Honest? I wouldn't be wearing this dress if he was honest! I wouldn't have fallen off the ledge if he was honest. I wouldn't have to cook that stinking Mung Chowder Gumbo if he was honest!!

KATE. How ungrateful! What kind of a best friend are you, anyway? I don't know why I let you take advantage of me.

LESLIE. Wait a minute. Wait a cotton-picking minute! You made the advances on me! I was an innocent best friend until you threw yourself at me. You came after me!

KATE. I felt sorry for you!

LESLIE. You loved every minute of it!

KATE. I can fake practically anything.

LESLIE. You want to fake a punch in the nose?

KATE. Leslie, stop. This isn't the time or the place. Connie isn't any wiser. Why don't you just go back to her?

LESLIE. I'd love to, but Connie doesn't even care about me. She's been ignoring me for weeks. That's probably why I was such an easy mark.

KATE. She wouldn't be coming over here if she didn't care about you.

LESLIE. You think so?

KATE. Of course I do.

LESLIE. But I can't just forget what happened between us. You know what I mean.

KATE. (*Holding his face in her hands.*) You'll get over it. Can we be friends?

LESLIE. (*Puts arms around her.*) Sure. You're right. It's better this way. Can I give you one final kiss goodbye?

KATE. If it'll make you happy.

LESLIE. Thanks.

(LESLIE *and* KATE *awkwardly kiss. Not with the passion they had in Act One, but a farewell kiss.* JON *walks in from the front door.* KATE *and* LESLIE *freeze in horror.* JON *stares with an open mouth.*)

JON. I don't believe this! My girlfriend and my wife! (JON *flings the catered food trays out the door, as a prelude of what's to come.*)

CURTAIN

ACT THREE

AS CURTAIN RISES, we find it is but moments later. KATE & LESLIE *are backing away in terror, as* JON *stalks them.* LESLIE *cannot speak.*

KATE. It's not what you think.

JON. What do I think, Kate?

KATE. You think Leslie and I were kissing.

JON. What were you doing?

KATE. We were kissing.

JON. That's what I thought.

KATE. Leslie, don't just stand there. Say something!

LESLIE. Jon, I frlaghh . . . brghahh . . .

JON. If you think your sinusses are bad now, just wait until I get through with your mucus membranes!

LESLIE. It's not what you think! Well, it is what you think but it's not what you think.

JON. Don't start on that again. What were you two doing?

LESLIE. I was checking her mouth for pyorrhea.

JON. What were you two doing?

LESLIE. I didn't touch her. Only her lips.

JON. Only her lips? That still qualifies as a violation. Now, stand still and fight like a man.

LESLIE. Is that any way to talk to your wife?

JON. Stand still.

KATE. Don't fight. Both of you, stop it!

LESLIE. I'm all for stopping it. Tell him to stop it!

JON. Let's discuss this like adults before I squeeze your head like a melon. Stop jumping around.

LESLIE. No chance, pal. I don't trust you.

JON. I've always trusted you.

LESLIE. Yeah and look where that got you.

JON. Stand still!

LESLIE. You better not touch me. Your mother might walk in here.

JON. If she does, she'll find my wife lying limp under the coffee table.

KATE. Jon, you can't beat up every problem that comes along.

LESLIE. He doesn't. He only beats up half of them. He lies to the other half.

KATE. What kind of flowers do you want on the casket, Leslie?

JON. Wait a second. How long has this been going on?

LESLIE. What was that?

JON. How long has this been going on?

LESLIE. Catchy title. You lought to write songs.

JON. How long has this been going on?

LESLIE. How what?

JON. How long?!!

LESLIE. So long.

(LESLIE *runs off into the bea,.   *ATE blocks* JON *from following. As she speaks, ,ıvıAN enters from the kitchen.*)

KATE. Jon, listen to me.

VIVIAN. Leslie? What am I supposed to do with that mess in there? That stuff is curdling!

KATE. Get off the battlefield, Mrs. Trachtman. We'll be in in a minute.

VIVIAN. I didn't fly in all the way from Chicago to eat curdled gumbo! (VIVIAN *exits back into the kitchen.*)

KATE. Now, Jon, don't say anything until I'm finished. It's true. Leslie and I have been fooling around behind your back for about a week now. But it's because I was feeling neglected. You've been so busy. I guess I was getting back at you for not spending any time with me. And you can't blame Leslie because I dragged him into this. He was in a very vulnerable state of mind. He didn't think that Connie loved him anymore and he needed somebody. We realized how wrong it was and we even tried to stop it before it went anywhere. We're very sorry. We didn't mean to hurt you. When you walked in, we had just decided to call the whole thing off and although you saw us kissing, we weren't really kissing. Do you understand? I love you very much and I still want to marry you. Please forgive me.

JON. I forgive you.

KATE. You're kidding. Oh Jon, thank you.

JON. I can't blame you for turning to someone else. I've been so busy finagling money and cheating the government, that I have ignored you.

KATE. Let's tell Leslie.

JON. Wait a minute. Let me finish. I forgive you, but I can't necessarily forget what went on here. If I was ignoring you, you could have mentioned it.

KATE. I tried, but you were never here.

JON. You could've left a note.

KATE. Are you saying that we're finished?

JON. We'll see.

KATE. "We'll see?" I said I was sorry.

JON. How do I know the next time you're feeling lonely, you won't start it up again?

KATE. I'll leave a note. I promise.

JON. Not good enough.

KATE. I said I apologize. You're wrong. I'll be loyal. I'll make you trust me again. Just say we'll always stay together.

JON. You know I love you Katie. If I believe I can trust you again, then . . . we'll see.

KATE. Oh, thank you. (*The DOORBELL rings.*)

JON. Boy, a hot dog stand would clean up here. We'll finish our discussion later.

KATE. Are you still going to squeeze Leslie's head like a melon?

JON. I promise I won't. Now, go help my mother before she squeezes your head like a melon. I'll get rid of our guest.

(KATE *exits into the kitchen.* JON *opens the door and in walks* CONNIE. *She is attractive, blonde and a talker.*)

JON. Connie!

CONNIE. Jon, I'm sorry I'm late.

JON. Connie . . .

CONNIE. Oh Jon, I don't know what to do. He doesn't see me for a week. He doesn't call me for a week. And why? Why? I was never anything but a joy to be around. You hear that? A joy! I shared the same interests that he did. We had wonderful times together. We laughed. We cried. Suddenly, for no reason—out of the blue—he says he's changed. He says, "things are different" for him. Well answer me this: What's changed? What's different for him? What is so different for him? Where is he? (LESLIE *sneaks into the room to see if the coast is clear.*)

LESLIE. Connie?

CONNIE. Leslie? Is that you?

LESLIE. Yes. Yes it is. Oh, Connie, I wish you didn't have to see me like this.

CONNIE. Where've you been?

LESLIE. I just came out of a closet.

CONNIE. You just came out of a what?

JON. Leslie . . .

LESLIE. Well, I have to go now. (LESLIE *backs off, terrified of* JON. CONNIE *tries to sort out what is going on.*)

CONNIE. He just came out of a closet?!

(FLOYD *stirs on the couch.* JON *begins speaking before he even thinks about it.*)

JON. Yes, Connie. It's true. Leslie likes to dress up in

women's clothing. He's wanted to come out of the closet for a while, but he didn't want to hurt you. He still cares for you Connie. Oh, it was a sad sight. I returned home from the supermarket one day and there was Leslie, in a black lingerie, dancing on the coffee table.

CONNIE. Omigod. What did I do to him? I'll admit that I've been domineering and bossy, but did I drive him to this?

JON. I'm afraid so. Your dominance must have forced it out. I knew he had these tendencies back in college. The panty-raids were always a little more of a pleasure to him than any of the other guys. We never knew what the reason was, until we realized he never returned the panties he raided.

CONNIE. Oh, Jon. I love him. I didn't mean to do this. What can I do?

JON. Nothing, Connie. Nothing. It'd probably be best if you just forget about him and let him die a natural death.

CONNIE. You don't die from it, do you?

JON. Only in a few rare cases. I'll do what I can for him. You just run along. (JON *notices* FLOYD *stir again.*)

CONNIE. No. I'm staying until he's well again.

JON. Look. Connie, you can't stay. See that man on the couch? I don't want him to see you.

CONNIE. Who is he?

JON. He's one of the men from the home.

CONNIE. The home?

JON. Yes. And there's another one in the kitchen who can't see you either.

CONNIE. Why not? What will they do to me?

JON. They'll arrest you for making Leslie go crazy. You'd better hide upstairs in my bedroom until they leave.

CONNIE. They'll arrest me? All right. Is he safe to be around? You know, up there?

JON. Don't worry about Leslie. I'm sure he'll just stay in his closet. But just to be safe, hide your make-up kit.

CONNIE. Okay.

(CONNIE *cautiously exits.* FLOYD *stirs again.* VIVIAN *enters from the kitchen, calling back in to* KATE.)

VIVIAN. Just stir it! That's what Leslie keeps telling me!

JON. I think Mr. Spinner's coming around.

VIVIAN. I wish I'd slept through the whole afternoon. What a disgrace! And what's worse is she's lazy. Kate and I did all the cooking. Yoo-hoo. Floyd, wake up.

JON. What are you doing, mom? Here, let me give you a hand.

VIVIAN. I can walk by myself, thank you. (VIVIAN *reaches* FLOYD *and sits beside him. She stares into his face.*) Boy, he's really tied one on! (VIVIAN *takes the cheese to wake him and grinds it into his face. He still does not awaken.* JON *catches the end of the cheese bit, preoccupied with what's upstairs.*)

JON. Let me get some water. (JON *gets some water from the bar.* VIVIAN *begins tapping* FLOYD's *face lightly.*)

VIVIAN. Floyd! Mr. Spinner! Mr. I.R.S. man! (VIVIAN *starts to slap his face.*) Oh, I've always wanted to do that to the Internal Revenue Service. (VIVIAN *begins slappng him broadly with glee.*) This is fun! And here's for auditing me in 1962! (VIVIAN *gives one big slap, which starts to bring him around.* JON *finally reaches her with the water.*)

JON. Mom! Here. (JON *hands* VIVIAN *the water and she hits* FLOYD *with it. He springs awake.*)

FLOYD. Wha . . . wha . . . where am I?

JON. Are you all right?

FLOYD. (*Stands up.*) Oh yes. I'm . . . oh. Oh! My head! What's on my head?

JON. Nothing. There's nothing on your head.

VIVIAN. It's the liquor striking back. See that? That's why I never drink.

FLOYD. Oh my . . . what's this lump on my head?

VIVIAN. Don't look at me. I only slapped him in the face.

JON. You've both gotten out of hand. Mr. Spinner, I

think dinner has been ruined. So, you'd better go home now. All the business for the day has been settled, hasn't it?

FLOYD. Yes. But what about the Mung Chowder Gumbo?

JON. You'll probably pass it on the stairs.

FLOYD. Oh, forget it, then. I'll go home. Where's my hat? (JON *retrieves it and planks it on* FLOYD's *head*.)

JON. Here you go, Mr. Spinner. Thanks for dropping by today.

FLOYD. (*Wincing in pain.*) I think I'll carry it. Thank you. It's been a delight knowing you, Mrs. Trachtman. Mr. Trachtman, please say goodbye to Leslie for me. And your girlfriend too. Here's my card. Just in case she changes her mind. Tell her my wife works until three Monday through Thursday and plays bridge Wednesday nights. Bye, bye. (FLOYD *exits, minus his briefcase*.)

JON. Finally, mom. Now can I explain what's been going on here today?

VIVIAN. What am I, stupid? Huh? I know damn well what's been going on here today. The I.R.S. man comes, so you and the cheap tramp pretend to be married and save yourselves some money. Well, I played along. And now I'll go to hell with the rest of you. Where's my suitcases? I'm leaving!

JON. No! You don't understand anything.

VIVIAN. Don't you talk to me. You're a disgrace to your father and myself. You aren't our son! Your poor father. He's rolling around in his grave right now, saying, "We've failed, Vivian. Our son is a failure." (VIVIAN *begins looking all over for her bags*.) Sodom and Gomorrah. Remember that story? Where're my bags?! God's going to destroy New York City because of you and your little friends. Forget the damn bags, I'm going! (VIVIAN *storms to the door*.)

JON. Mom. Give me a chance to explain!

VIVIAN. Couldn't you have married at least one of them,

to humor me? No. You like the idea of your father burning in hell for producing a moralless degenerate. Well, I hope you're satisfied! (VIVIAN *slams the door behind her and exits, leaving* JON *slumped against the door, a broken man.*)

JON. Mom! . . . (KATE *slowly re-enters from the kitchen. She crosses to him and puts her arms around him.*)

KATE. Oh, Jon.

JON. Don't say anything, Kate. I had it coming to me. Try and cheat the government and look what happens. (JON *releases* KATE *to continue his tirade.*) Try to get enough money to simply survive and look what happens. They get me. They don't know I did anything, but they got me anyway. I may have enough money to eat as a result of this, but is it worth it? Look what else I got along with it. My girlfriend and my best friend almost ran off together. My mother has disowned me. I just missed getting thrown out of my apartment. Leslie almost killed himself out on the ledge. And you want to know the worst part? Guilt. I'm full of guilt. I've lied. I've deceived a sweet little man who wouldn't harm a fly. I've deceived my mother. She thinks she's a failure. My father's rolling around in his grave, wrinkling his suit. All because of me. I'm full of guilt. Guilt. Guilt. Guilt. It's going to hang over me for the rest of my life. Now I know how Richard Nixon feels. Poor guy.

KATE. Boy, you must feel guilty.

(*The DOORBELL rings.* KATE *leaves* JON *and answers the door. In walks* JANSEN *with a pile of all the things* LESLIE *dropped off the ledge.*)

JANSEN. Somebody drop these?

JON. No. What makes you think they're Kate's?

JANSEN. Mrs. Gill brought them to me. She said she was out sunbathing on her terrace when out of the sky came a flying woman.

JON. A flying woman?

JANSEN. She swears she's telling the truth. The shock put her dog in a coma. I saw him. He's just lying there with a big bulge in his throat. Anyhow, she must've been pretty upset. She ran down to my apartment without a stitch on. It's the first time a pink elephant ever knocked before coming in.

JON. So, what makes you think those things are ours?

JANSEN. Your apartment is the only one above hers. I deduced that somebody must've thrown them out the window when I went upstairs to search the bedrooms before.

JON. That doesn't explain the flying woman.

JANSEN. She probably used that as an excuse to come in my apartment naked.

KATE. Mr. Jansen, nobody lives here but Jon and Leslie.

JANSEN. That's what everybody keeps saying, but where is Leslie? I haven't seen him around much today.

JON. Oh. You mean, where is he?

JANSEN. Yeah. Where is he? I don't suppose he moved out so she could move in.

KATE. I beg your pardon.

JON. Certainly not.

(LESLIE, *stripped of his make-up and out of drag, enters.*)

LESLIE. Did you see my . . . oh, hi Mr. Jansen.

JANSEN. There you are. Where've you been all day?

LESLIE. Me? I've been resting. I haven't been myself all day.

JANSEN. Why didn't I see you when I searched around up there?

LESLIE. I was under the covers.

JANSEN. I looked under the covers.

LESLIE. Then I was under the bed.

JANSEN. You gave me permission to search the apartment whenever I wanted to. Didn't you?

LESLIE. Yes, I did. But let's not make a habit of it.

JON. We do like our privacy.

JANSEN. I understand. This will be the last time. I promise. I kinda got a hunch.

LESLIE. Very well, then. Search away!

JON. Leslie!

LESLIE. What? We have nothing to hide. Go ahead, Mr. Jansen. Leave no stone unturned!

JANSEN. All right, I'll do that. Pardone. (JANSEN *exits with a flair*.)

JON. Leslie, you idiot! I could kill you!

LESLIE. Didn't Kate explain everything? Please don't kill me.

KATE. Everything's fine, Leslie.

JON. I'm not really going to kill you.

LESLIE. Good. I'd hate to die with red tights on.

JON. Why did you let him go up there?

LESLIE. Don't worry. I stuffed my dresses in the pillow cases.

JON. I'm not talking about your clothes!

KATE. What are you talking about?

LESLIE. There's no one up there!

JON. Oh no?

(CONNIE *screams from Off-Left*.)

LESLIE. Who is that?

(JANSEN *enters with* CONNIE *flung over his shoulder*.)

CONNIE. Don't hurt me. I didn't mean to do anything!

LESLIE. Hi Connie.

CONNIE. What are you going to do to me?

JANSEN. Quiet you! You're in enough hot water. All right, you two wise guys, what's this? Huh?

LESLIE. That's my girlfriend, Connie.

JANSEN. I'll go retrieve a certain document and we'll see

what happens next. (JANSEN *exits with* CONNIE *kicking and screaming all the way out.*)

CONNIE. I'm sorry, Leslie! Forgive me! Where are you taking me? Leslie, I love you! I'm sorry! (*They are gone.*)

LESLIE. She loves me. Did you hear that, Kate? She really does love me!

KATE. Why was she apologizing?

JON. She thinks Jansen's from a rest home and he's taking her away.

LESLIE. Why does she think that?

JON. Because I told her that. I'd almost gotten rid of her when you sashayed in here. I had to tell her something.

LESLIE. What did you tell her?

JON. I told her that you like dressing up in women's clothes.

LESLIE. You told her that I what?!

JON. Like dressing up in women's clothes.

LESLIE. I heard you! (*The DOORBELL rings.*)

JON. Who's there?

FLOYD. It's me. Mr. Spinner!

JON. Just a minute. Leslie's getting dressed.

LESLIE. Leslie is not getting dressed! Leslie has had it with getting dressed!

JON. Leslie, please. This is the last time I'll ever ask you.

LESLIE. Tell him I'm out shopping.

JON. I just told him you were getting dressed.

LESLIE. Then tell him I'm out shopping for dresses.

JON. Leslie, dammit. Go put a dress on!

LESLIE. I'm not wearing any more make-up.

JON. I don't care what you put on your face. Just put a dress on.

LESLIE. Okay. Get rid of him.

(LESLIE *exits.* JON *opens the door and in walks* FLOYD. *He is walking on eggs with a splitting headache.*)

FLOYD. I feel very foolish. I'm sorry to bother you again, but I . . . I left my briefcase here. I can't very well tie up all the loose ends in your case without my papers and forms.

JON. You're absolutely right. I'll just go get your briefcase and you can be on your way. (JON *quickly exits to the kitchen.*)

FLOYD. Fine. Thank you.

KATE. Don't you come near me.

FLOYD. I haven't the energy.

KATE. Good. We're out of scotch bottles.

JON. (*Re-enters with the briefcase.*) Here we go. Thanks again for everything, Mr. Spinner. Let me walk you to the elevator.

(JON *opens the door and before they can exit, in walks* VIVIAN *and* ARNOLD GRUNION; *a shady character, in his late forties. He wears a trenchcoat and keeps looking over his shoulder. He carries a beat-up old briefcase.*)

VIVIAN. Hello, dear. I'm back. Meet Arnold Grunion. Mr. Grunion, meet my son Jon. Floyd Spinner—a good friend of mine. And that's Kate. Jon's . . . sister-in-law, right Mr. Spinner?

FLOYD. That's right. Sister-in-law.

KATE. What's going on?

JON. Mom, what happened? Why did you come back?

VIVIAN. I bring wonderful news. Where's Leslie?

(LESLIE *sweeps into the room, wearing a red Maribu-feathered nightgown. His hair is tied up in a kerchief and his face is smeared totally with cold cream.*)

LESLIE. Why, welcome back, Mrs. Trachtman.

VIVIAN. Oh, no. You call me "mom," Leslie.

LESLIE. Okay. Mom.

VIVIAN. What's all over your face?

JON. It's cold cream, mom. Leslie has a bad skin problem. Don't you, Leslie?

LESLIE. That's right, mom.

JON. Wait a minute. Why the change of heart?

VIVIAN. I met Mr. Grunion in the subway.

LESLIE. Oh. Picked up a guy, huh mom?

VIVIAN. I did not. Mr. Grunion, meet Jon's Leslie.

GRUNION. Charmed.

JON. Mom, can I speak with you for a moment?

GRUNION. Oh. I'll need your signature here, Mr. Trachtman. (GRUNION *pulls out some document that* JON *unwittingly signs.*)

JON. I think I'd like to know what's going on.

GRUNION. Thank you. Leslie, sign right here, please.

FLOYD. Oh no. She can't. Leslie has to sign things in the kitchen or she'll go blind.

GRUNION. No kidding. Shall we, Leslie?

LESLIE. I don't know. I guess we shall. Just don't try anything funny.

GRUNION. Don't worry about that.

(LESLIE *and* GRUNION *exit to the kitchen.* JON *is totally baffled.*)

JON. Mom, what is happening?

VIVIAN. I'll admit Mr. Grunion is a little on the shady side, but it's all perfectly legal.

JON. Legal? What's all perfectly legal?

VIVIAN. Mr. Grunion has agreed to marry you both tonight. I can't bear the thought of you two living together another second.

FLOYD. What? They're not married?

JON. Mom! Mr. Spinner, don't listen to her! She doesn't know what she's saying.

VIVIAN. Oh. I thought you were in the kitchen.

FLOYD. Jon and Leslie aren't married?

VIVIAN. (*After a pause.*) That's right, Mr. Spinner. Jon and Leslie are unwed. In my eyes. You see, they eloped. I was never present at their wedding, so in my eyes they aren't married.

FLOYD. Oh. I see. This is a remarriage.

VIVIAN. Yes. Something like that.

JON. Thanks mom.

VIVIAN. You owe me one.

JON. You see, Mr. Spinner, Leslie and I were going to be remarried in about two weeks.

VIVIAN. But now that I'm here, we'll do it tonight. This will ease my mind and your father will finally rest in peace.

JON. Mom, couldn't this wait?

VIVIAN. It cannot. I will not allow this smut to continue one more night.

FLOYD. This is splended. May I volunteer to be a witness? I just love these remarriages.

KATE. Oh brother.

VIVIAN. Certainly. We'll be glad to have you, won't we Jon?

JON. Yes. These are tears of joy, Mr. Spinner.

VIVIAN. (*To* KATE.) And you, young lady. I hope this will put an end to the goings on between you and my son.

KATE. I would never date a married man. Just ask Mr. Spinner.

FLOYD. (*Rubbing head.*) She's not kidding.

VIVIAN. Good. From now on, it's Jon and Leslie til death do they part.

JON. Boy, I can't thank you enough, mom.

(*The DOORBELL rings.* FLOYD *quickly answers.* CONNIE *rushes in.*)

CONNIE. Quick. Shut the door. I think I lost him. (FLOYD *and* CONNIE *slam the door shut and lean on it.* FLOYD *has an ear to the door.*)

FLOYD. I don't hear anyone.

VIVIAN. Who is this person?

JON. Connie, a good friend of Leslie's. Connie, these are the people I told you about before.

CONNIE. Oh no. Am I safe here?

FLOYD. Of course you are. You're just in time for the wedding.

CONNIE. What does he mean? You're getting married Jon?

VIVIAN. Of course he is. How do you do, Connie. I'm Jon's mother.

CONNIE. Do you work in the home too?

VIVIAN. Of course I work in the home. What do you think I am?

CONNIE. You won't hurt me, will you?

VIVIAN. I'll try and control myself.

FLOYD. Shouldn't we be getting on with the wedding?

KATE. I don't see why we should rush into this thing tonight.

VIVIAN. Look, you hussy, Jon and Leslie are getting married and nothing you say or do is going to stop it.

CONNIE. Jon and Leslie?

VIVIAN. Any objections?

CONNIE. Of course. But if you think this is what's best for Leslie, then I agree with all my heart.

VIVIAN. Well, I do.

JON. Oh, brother.

CONNIE. Then I'm all for it. I hope it helps. May I stay?

FLOYD. Of course you may. The more the merrier. Have a seat, Connie.

VIVIAN. Mr. Grunion! We're ready! Look at Jon, everybody. He's tongue-tied. Isn't that sweet?

GRUNION. (*Enters from the kitchen holding the document and his pen.*) We've come up with a little resistance.

LESLIE. *(Bee-lines in at* JON.*)* That's a marriage license!

VIVIAN. That's right, Leslie. Now, sign it.

LESLIE. I will not! Jon, that's a marriage license! He's a Justice of the Peace! Connie, help me.

CONNIE. Sign it, Leslie. And it'll help you. Come on, it'll do you good.

LESLIE. Jon! Kate!

KATE. Jon, do something.

JON. Mr. Spinner from the I.R.S. is going to be a witness, Leslie. I guess you'd better sign it.

CONNIE. Yes. Sign it, Leslie.

LESLIE. Oh, shut up, you. This is legal?

FLOYD. Yes. Now, come on, Leslie. You've been outvoted. Believe me, you'll feel better if you do.

CONNIE. Listen to him, Leslie. He knows what he's talking about.

KATE. Jon.

JON. Leslie. Mr. Spinner, from the I.R.S. would like you to sign it. Wouldn't you, sir?

FLOYD. Yes, I would.

JON. Then sign it Leslie.

LESLIE. *(Begru.'g.ngly signs his name, mumbling to* JON.*)* You son of a bitch!

VIVIAN. It'll make an honest woman of you.

CONNIE. That's right.

VIVIAN. Go ahead, Mr. Grunion.

GRUNION. Dearly beloved, we are gathered here today to join together Jonathon Frederick Trachtman and Leslie Carroll Arthur in holy matrimony. If there be anyone present who has just cause or reason why these two should not be married, speak now or forever hold your peace.

(There is a moment of silence. LESLIE *can stand no more.)*

LESLIE. I can't do it! Me! I have just cause and I want to let go of my b—

JON. Leslie! Don't ruin it!

LESLIE. I've done a lot for you, but I'm not doing this! In the first place, Mr. Spinner, I am not married to Jon, nor have I ever been.

FLOYD. What?

JON. You ruined it, Leslie.

LESLIE. Mrs. Trachtman, for eight years I've roomed with Jon. And many times over those years, Jon has asked me to do some very bizarre, outlandish things. And for eight years, I've done every bizarre and outlanddish thing he's ever asked me to do. I've bent over backwards.

VIVIAN. I don't care to hear the sordid details of your sex life!

LESLIE. For eight years I've never complained. I've never refused. And why? Because Jon's my best friend. That's why. We've been through a lot together and he's been very good to me. But this time, I'm forced to pretend I'm his wife. That alone is humiliating enough. But I did it. I felt I owed it to him. So, I did it. But what went along with pretending I was his wife? I'm forced to wear clothes so small, they were practically put on intraveinously. I'm forced to cook Mung Chowder Gumbo when I don't even know what the hell a mung looks like! I'm forced out on a ledge five stories up, which I fall off. I land on Miss Goodyear 1947 and I'm almost ripped to shreds by an arthritic German shepherd named Coco. And finally I come back up here to find out Connie's been told that I'm being put away in a rubber room. This much I did. Even though everyone was told that I was going blind, have bunyans, have a bad skin problem and have a hygiene disorder! And why did I feel I owed this to Jon? Because of one yes. That's why. He said, "Let me do your taxes" and I said yes. All of this for one stinking yes. But now. Now. I'm told to sign a marriage license and spend the rest of my life being referred to as the "little woman." Well, this time, I refuse. And you want to know why? You want to know why, Jon? I'll tell you why. Because I don't feel like it.

That's why. What do you think of that?! (*There is a moment of silence as this all sinks in.*)

VIVIAN. I'm sorry you've had a rough day. Now get over here and marry my son.

LESLIE. (*Rips off the kerchief.*) Don't you understand? I am not a woman! (LESLIE *removes the socks and the nightgown.*) I have never been a woman. I hate the color pink. I have never used a creme rinse. I've never gone to a restroom with a group! Jon wanted to save money from the Internal Revenue Service, so he lied and said we were married. Well, we're not married. We aren't even going together!

GRUNION. This is still costing you ten bucks, lady.

VIVIAN. Why the hell didn't anyone tell me before?

JON. It got out of hand. We tried a couple of times, but you were so smashed we finally gave up.

CONNIE. Does this mean I'm not going to be arrested?

LESLIE. Of course not, Connie. That was another one of Jon's stories.

CONNIE. Whew! Welcome back, Leslie. I missed you.

JON. Are you mad, mom?

VIVIAN. I think the word is "relieved," dear.

KATE. Mrs. Trachtman, I'm the girl who's going to marry Jon in two weeks.

VIVIAN. Thand God. At least you look human.

FLOYD. Tax fraud. (*An uncomfortable silence prevails.*) I've never seen anyone go to such complicated lengths before. I must congratulate you two. You almost got away with it.

JON. Mr. Spinner, I don't know what to say.

LESLIE. Do we go to jail now?

FLOYD. You should. But I'm not going to report you.

JON. You're not going to report us?

FLOYD. Goodness, no. You're the first people that have ever been nice to me. I couldn't report you. I've never had a better time in my life.

LESLIE. But we broke the law.

FLOYD. That's all right, too.

LESLIE. It is?

FLOYD. Yes. I've got seven imaginary kids.

LESLIE. You do?

JON. All this time, you've been committing tax fraud yourself?

FLOYD. Sure. If I ever get caught, I'll report you and we can all go to jail together.

JANSEN. (*Enters with his passkey, holding a crumpled lease. He stares at* LESLIE. *Glances at beer. Back to* LESLIE. *Puts beer down and continues.*) I found it. I found it. (*To* CONNIE.) What did you run away for? I asked you to wait in my bedroom until I came to get you.

CONNIE. You just answered your own question.

VIVIAN. What is it you were looking for?

JANSEN. Their lease. It took a while to find. I had to move a lot of junk around. But I found it. Wrapped around an egg salad sandwich. I think it was egg salad. Tasted like it. Read this. Right here. No men and women may live together unless they're married.

JON. Then that has nothing to do with me.

LESLIE. That's right.

JON. Mr. Grunion, how would you like to earn another ten dollars?

GRUNION. I'm not going anywhere.

KATE. Is that a proposal?

JON. You bet it is. I believe you, I trust you and I love you very much. Will you marry me?

KATE. How bad do you need the money, Mr. Grunion? Of course I'll marry you. If you really want me.

JON. Of course I do, Moonpie. (JON *and* KATE *kiss.* CONNIE *elbows* LESLIE.)

CONNIE. Leslie.

LESLIE. Yes, Connie?

CONNIE. Pay Mr. Grunion ten dollars.

LESLIE. How come?

CONNIE. We're getting married!

LESLIE. Oh. I'd love to. (CONNIE *and* LESLIE *kiss*.)

GRUNION. Anybody else? My rates drop for groups.

JANSEN. What the hell is going on here?

VIVIAN. A double wedding.

FLOYD. Isn't love wonderful, Mr. Jansen?

JANSEN. What are you asking me for? Has Mrs. Gill been up here blabbing her mouth off again?

FLOYD. Who?

JANSEN. Skip it.

JON. Katie, now that we're getting married, how many kids do you want to have?

KATE. I don't know. Why?

JON. I was just thinking . . . for next year's tax return, why don't we adopt Leslie and Connie.

LESLIE. Oh, no you don't. I'm not wearing diapers for you.

JON. Come on, Leslie . . .

(*Witty ad lib patter as the lights come down.*)

THE END

PROPERTY LIST

ACT ONE—Scene 1
Bar
    2 half-filled drinks
    Ice bucket, with ice
    Scotch
    Bourbon
    Vodka
    Water pitcher
    Glasses

Upper Right Wall
    Girlie calendar

Stage Left Chair
    KATE's blazer
    KATE's pocketbook
Stage Left Table
    Telephone
Off-Stage Right (Kitchen)
    Dried flowers in vase (JON)
    Apron (LESLIE)
    Limburger cheese on paper plate (KATE)
    Towel (KATE)
    12 empty beer cans (JANSEN)
    Wooden spoon (VIVIAN)
Off-Stage Left (Bedrooms)
    Compact (LESLIE)
    Mirror (LESLIE)
    Cold cream (LESLIE)
    All of LESLIE's costumes
Off-Stage Upper Right (Hallway)
    Music book (JON)
    Take-out food (JON)
    Ripped copy of LESLIE's yellow chiffon dress (LESLIE)

Telegram (JANSEN)
Passkeys (JANSEN)
Beer can (JANSEN)
Catcher's mask (JANSEN)
Lease (JANSEN)
3 extra dresses (KATE)
Cigarettes (FLOYD)
Briefcase (FLOYD)
Legal form papers (FLOYD)
Pens (FLOYD)
2 large suitcases (VIVIAN)
Beat-up briefcase (ARNOLD)
Marriage license (ARNOLD)
Pen (ARNOLD)
Off-Stage Upper Right (Hallway)
    I.D. containing birth certificate and social security card
    Pencils
    Breakaway bottle
    Box containing: 2 bras, 2 hats, mink stole, 2 lace throw
       pillows, 2 pair of pantyhose, clothesline, pocketbook,
       3 spare dresses, adomizer (filled with water), McCall's
       Magazine, pointed bathing cap, blue sash.

ACT ONE—SCENE 2
Coffee Table
    Set I.D.
    Set pencils
Upper Right Wall
    Flip girlie calendar, revealing "HOME SWEET
    HOME" sign
Strike Telegram
Stage Left Chair
    Set box of props

ACT TWO
Bar
    Set breakaway bottle

Coffee Table
  Set Scotch bottle and 2 filled glasses

ACT THREE
Strike Take-Out Food
Upper Right Prop Table
  Re-set LESLIE's ledge props (JANSEN)

COSTUME PLOT

LESLIE ARTHUR: (NOTE: LESLIE's changes will be quicker and easier if his tights and boxer shorts are worn underneath everything)

  ACT ONE—SCENE 1
    Blue V-neck
    Jeans
    White socks
    Step in suede shoes
  ACT ONE—SCENE 2
    Remove V-neck
    Add flannel bathrobe
        into
    Stuffed bra
    Red wig
    Fuzzy pink slippers
    Floral bathrobe
    Kerchief in hair
        into
    Screaming yellow chiffon dress (tight)
    Remove kerchief
    Long black cocktail gloves
    Black heels (Feet should hang over about 6″)
    Add lipstick (red)
    Add eye shadow (blue)
    Add eye-liner
    Add mole on cheek

  ACT TWO
    Same
        into
    Ripped replica of yellow chiffon dress
    Lose wig
    Lose left glove

Lose right shoe
        into
Same
Add pointed bathing cap
Add blue sash

ACT THREE
Same
        into
Jeans
Bathrobe
Step in suede shoes
Remove make-up
Keep bra under
        into
Red Maribu-feathered nightgown
Big shower cap
Fuzzy pink slippers
Pink gloves
Add cold cream on face
Keep bra under

JON TRACHTMAN:
ACT ONE—SCENE 1
Tan pants
White shirt
Checked jacket
Brown tie
Step in brown shoes
        into
Jeans
Pullover
Same shoes

ACT ONE—SCENE 2
Same as first entrance
ACT TWO
Same

ACT THREE
Same

KATE DENNIS:
ACT ONE—SCENE 1
Pastel blouse
Tight jeans
Boots
Blazer
Pocketbook
ACT ONE—SCENE 2
Maroon blouse with spaghetti-string straps
Print skirt
Heels
Pocketbook
ACT TWO
Same
ACT THREE
Same

FLOYD SPINNER:
ACT ONE—SCENE 2
Brown suit
White shirt
Black shoes
White socks
Print tie
Round-framed glasses
Hat
Cigarettes in pocket
ACT TWO
Same
ACT THREE
Same

VIVIAN TRACHTMAN:
ACT ONE—SCENE 2
Tweed suit

Matching hat
Matching gloves
Heels
Purse
ACT TWO
Same
ACT THREE
Same

MR. JANSEN:
ACT ONE—SCENE 1
Khaki pants
Grubby Guinea T-Shirt
White socks
Work shoes
Handkerchief in back pocket
ACT TWO
Same
Add catcher's mask
ACT THREE
Same as first entrance

CONNIE:
ACT THREE
Blue-white striped dress
White blazer
Heels
Pocketbook

ARNOLD GRUNION:
ACT THREE
Trenchcoat
White shirt
Brown pants
White socks
Brown shoes

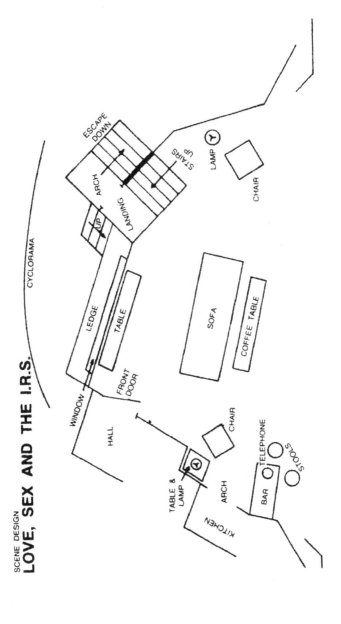

SCENE DESIGN
LOVE, SEX AND THE I.R.S.

CYCLORAMA

ESCAPE DOWN

ARCH

STAIRS UP

LANDING

LAMP

CHAIR

UP

LEDGE

TABLE

SOFA

COFFEE TABLE

WINDOW

FRONT DOOR

HALL

CHAIR

TABLE & LAMP

ARCH

TELEPHONE

BAR

STOOLS

KITCHEN

COCKEYED
William Missouri Downs

Comedy / 3m, 1f / Unit Set

Phil, an average nice guy, is madly in love with the beautiful Sophia. The only problem is that she's unaware of his existence. He tries to introduce himself but she looks right through him. When Phil discovers Sophia has a glass eye, he thinks that might be the problem, but soon realizes that she really can't see him. Perhaps he is caught in a philosophical hyperspace or dualistic reality or perhaps beautiful women are just unaware of nice guys. Armed only with a B.A. in philosophy, Phil sets out to prove his existence and win Sophia's heart. This fast moving farce is the winner of the HotCity Theatre's GreenHouse New Play Festival. The St. Louis Post-Dispatch called Cockeyed a clever romantic comedy, Talkin' Broadway called it "hilarious," while Playback Magazine said that it was "fresh and invigorating."

Winner!
of the HotCity Theatre GreenHouse New Play Festival

"Rocking with laughter...hilarious...polished and engaging work draws heavily on the age-old conventions of farce: improbable situations, exaggerated characters, amazing coincidences, absurd misunderstandings, people hiding in closets and barely missing each other as they run in and out of doors...full of comic momentum as Cockeyed hurtles toward its conclusion."
- Talkin' Broadway

NO SEX PLEASE, WE'RE BRITISH
Anthony Marriott and Alistair Foot

Farce / 7 m., 3 f. / Int.

A young bride who lives above a bank with her husband who is the assistant manager, innocently sends a mail order off for some Scandinavian glassware. What comes is Scandinavian pornography. The plot revolves around what is to be done with the veritable floods of pornography, photographs, books, films and eventually girls that threaten to engulf this happy couple. The matter is considerably complicated by the man's mother, his boss, a visiting bank inspector, a police superintendent and a muddled friend who does everything wrong in his reluctant efforts to set everything right, all of which works up to a hilarious ending of closed or slamming doors. This farce ran in London over eight years and also delighted Broadway audiences.

"Titillating and topical."
- "NBC TV"

"A really funny Broadway show."
- "ABC TV"

CPSIA information can be obtained
at www.ICGtesting.com
Printed in the USA
BVHW061324240820
587148BV00008B/204

9 780573 611964